A CONVERGENCE
OF BIRDS

A CONVERGENCE OF BIRDS

Original Fiction and Poetry Inspired by the Work of Joseph Cornell

Edited by

JONATHAN SAFRAN FOER

D.A.P.

D.A.P. / Distributed Art Publishers, Inc.

Published in the United States by
D.A.P. / Distributed Art Publishers, Inc.
155 Sixth Ave. 2nd Floor
New York NY 10013

Library of Congress Control Number 00-136539

Printed in Hong Kong

ISBN 1-891024-22-1 (Trade Edition)
ISBN 1-891024-30-2 (Limited Edition)

First Edition

Design and Typesetting: Anne Galperin
Production Manager: Craig Willis

Contents

ACKNOWLEDGMENTS

THIS BOOK WOULD NOT HAVE BEEN POSSIBLE without the tremendous knowledge and generosity of Jennifer Vorbach at C&M Arts, John Mason and Margaret Richardson at PaceWildenstein, Mary Anne Orszag at the Des Moines Art Center, and Geraldine Aramanda at the Menil Collection, all of whom bent over backward to make sure we were provided with what we needed (and didn't even know we needed). Their assistance was always prompt, thorough, and downright charitable. It is absolutely no exaggeration to say that this book would not have been possible without them.... Robert Lehrman has been the epitome of giving—as a collector and enthusiast nonpareil, and as a friend—and for this I am extremely grateful. Similarly, Lindy Bergman, the wonderful Lindy Bergman, deserves to have her name sung very loudly from some high place.... Thanks are also due to Russell Banks for his early encouragement and help, to James Seawright, for introducing me to the art of Joseph Cornell and for reminding me of the urgency of needing to know how things work, to the Greensfelders and Segals for giving me beautiful places to work and make phone calls, to DG, KE, MS, SC, KJ, JJ, MJV, JK, and RF for insisting on intangibles, and to the good people at D.A.P.—particularly Sharon Gallagher, Avery Lozada, and Craig Willis, who are nothing less than heroes (and virtuosos) of contemporary publishing.... I could never give enough thanks to all of the writers who contributed to this book. Their faith in the project was as extraordinary as the stories and poems they wrote for it. I hope that they are pleased with the results.... And I can only hope that this book would have pleased Joseph Cornell. His art has dramatically changed my life, given me a sense of purpose and directed joy, and shown me that certain feelings can be given certain embodiments. Thank you is not enough, so I hope to give more.... And finally, I thank my parents and my brothers, who continue to teach me that laughter is not secular, and that imagination is life.

RESPONSE AND CALL

LETTERS WERE WRITTEN. Stamps were licked, envelopes addressed, mailboxes fed like starving animals. "CHILDREN'S PRE-VIEW of the exhibition JOSEPH CORNELL—COLLAGES AND BOXES." It was to be his first museum show dedicated to children, and the last show of his life.

Hundreds went that spring, 1972. Many were entranced by Cornell's works (which were displayed only a few feet off of the ground), and many by the chocolate cake that was passed about on plastic platters. Some cried, some fell asleep on the parquet, and some left with "party favors"—complimentary posters, signed by Cornell.

Fifteen years later, a young woman received one of these posters in the mail. It was from an ex-lover she hadn't thought about since college. Just above Cornell's signature he had written: *I love this. You will love this.* When the young woman died in a car accident the following summer, the poster was rolled up and forgotten about.

1992: The young woman's brother asked a friend (who would, years later, become a friend of mine) if he would help him sift through a roomful of boxes in an Upstate storage facility. It was time to save what was worth saving and part with the rest. He couldn't do it alone. When they came upon the poster, both were surprised: the friend because of the rare artifact of his favorite artist's life, the brother because above the two pieces of handwriting (Cornell's signature and the love note), was a third—in shaky blue ink: *This belonged to Beatrice.* He didn't know if it had been written by his father, or mother, or by his sister herself. And because he was alone—his parents having passed away the previous winter, within a month of each other—there was no way to find out.

By the time I saw the poster—on an August 1995 visit to my friend's studio—there was another text: this one, like the first two, of known origin. The brother had written: *A gift of a gift of a gift.* "He needed to get rid of it," my friend told me. "It was that kind of gift." My friend had attached the poster to a large canvas, hoping to make good use of it in a painting he was working on for an upcoming show. In the brief conversation that ensued, I learned the history of the poster, and learned, for the first time, about Cornell, who was "not quite a Surrealist," and had "exhausted his medium, as all geniuses do."

That afternoon, following something between a whim and a premonition, I went to the New York Public Library and found the catalogue for MoMA's 1980 Cornell retrospective. On the withdraw card was a roster of names: those belonging to the eleven people who had already taken the book out that year. I remember Elena Salter, and I remember Donald Franks. I remember a Henry, a Theresa, a Jennifer and a James. Each name was written in a different script, each with a different pen, held by a different hand. I signed my name into the registry—as if the catalogue were a hotel, as if I expected to meet the eleven others in some metaphysical lobby—and took it home. My life began to change.

By the end of the summer, I was pursuing obscure references, tracking down essays about essays about essays. When the new school year began, I spent afternoons in the university art library, sifting through the precious few books that had Cornell images. I hunted for more images, more stories, and spent weekends in Manhattan's rare art book stores, flipping through the pages of limited edition gallery catalogues that I would never be able to afford. Of course I read Deborah Solomon's biography (dedicated to her husband, Kent Sepkowitz) when it came out in 1997, and even gave a copy of it to a girl I was then interested in. *I love this*, I wrote on the title page, and, *You will love this*. (What was the *this*? The biography? Cornell? The love of Cornell? Of gifts? Of inscriptions? The love of the beginning of love?) It wasn't until two years and hundreds of hours of research later—a quarter of a century after those first letters were sent out—that the seeds of the simple idea were planted: I must do something with my love—for Cornell, for my love of Cornell, for gifts, inscriptions and the beginning of love.

I began to write letters.

⊱━◆━◯━◆━⊰

Dear Mr. Foer:

Your letter, which covers a whole page, contains only one line about what you want: " . . . a story or poem that uses Joseph Cornell's bird boxes as the source of imaginative inspiration . . . (but) which need not make any explicit reference to either Cornell or the art itself . . ." Since I don't know what this means, since you mention no fee (is there one or not?), since the whole issue seems to be a question of getting contributions, for nothing, from various well-known people to suit your own ends (vague as they are), and since for some reason you seem to think I'd be "as excited about this project as [you] are," how can I say yes, even with the very best of wills?

This was one of the first responses I received. My father read it to me over the phone—I had given my permanent address in D.C., rather than my college address in New Jersey, thinking I could skirt at least the most obvious challenge to my legitimacy. I shook with excitement as he began the reading, and disgrace by the time he had finished. "What a jerk," he sighed, and I sighed: "Yeah." Although I wasn't sure just whom we were talking about.

The letter was troubling. Needlessly nasty, perhaps, but no less accurate for its tone. Sadly, I was inclined to agree with its author: my project was naive, ill-defined and blatantly unnecessary.

Naive in that I was completely unfamiliar with the publishing world and what it takes to put together a book. I had no agent, no prospective publisher, no notion of fees or photo permissions.

Ill-defined in that I knew I wanted to assemble a book of writing inspired by Cornell's bird boxes, but little else. Would the book be literature, art, or some combination of the two? Should the pieces be of approximately the same length? How many images would be reproduced, and how would such a book be designed?

Unnecessary in that there have been several excellent books about Cornell. Granted, none like the kind I had in mind, but non-existence is not sufficient grounds for creating something. Without knowing exactly what distinguished the book I was envisioning from those already published—save for the obvious: that mine would be fiction and poetry from a variety of sources—I couldn't well answer what should have been my original question: Why?

And yes, who the hell was I—unpublished college student, self-educated in art history, uneducated in book publishing—to ask for things from people I didn't know, with nothing to offer in exchange? The jerk was me.

And yet, when I somewhat reluctantly called in for messages the next day, my father said, "I have some good news." And there were two more pieces of good news the day after that, and two the following day. By the end of the week, seven writers had agreed— quite enthusiastically—to be part of the still-forming project, and within half a year, I had a nearly completed manuscript. Were those eager writers jerks?

No. They were believers. But not in me and my maladroit pro-posal. It wasn't my supplication they were responding to, it was Cornell's—not even Cornell's, but that of his boxes. The boxes called the writers in from great distances; they demanded the attention of those who had no attention to spare. "I'm going to be in Tunisia for the next few months," one author responded, "but I'd like to give this my best shot." Another wrote his story on note cards as he traveled through the Spanish countryside by train. Another while she was preparing for an Italian sabbatical.

The boxes moved questions of logistics to the backdrop. No one—save for that early respondent—asked about fees or agents or publishers. They didn't ask about these things because they weren't responding to me. Their responses predated my call. I was just lucky enough to intercept them.

>—+·+>·•○•·<+·+—<

Many of Cornell's most brilliant boxes were not intended for the museums in which they now reside. They were gifts, tokens of affec-tion—*I love this. You will love this.* He had them delivered to his favorite movie stars and authors. He handed them, personally, to his most loved ballerinas. And they were almost uniformly sent back. He was rejected, laughed at, and, in one unfortunate case, tackled.

But the boxes themselves—not his hopelessly romantic supplica-tion—survived. More than survived, they came to be considered among the most seminal works of twentieth-century art. Their call beckoned, and continues to beckon, curators, museum-goers, and so many artists and writers. *Their* call, not Cornell's. They became gifts of gifts of gifts of gifts—a cascade of gifts without fixed givers or receivers.

So what is it about Cornell's boxes that made him a world-famous artist, and allowed my inept proposal to take flight? The answer, of course, is inexhaustible—it changes with each viewing. I hope that a few of the many answers are in this book, which is neither an homage nor a festschrift, but an assemblage of letters. Other answers are with you. When you read these pages, when you look at the images, imagine the letter that you would write. How would it begin? Who would be the characters? What images would come to the fore? What feelings? What colors and shapes? And as the imaginative cloud begins to open itself over your head, ask yourself: To whom would you address such a letter? What would you use as the return address?

JONATHAN SAFRAN FOER
Jackson Heights, New York
September 2000

EMORY BEAR HANDS' BIRDS

Barry Lopez

MY NAME IS JULIO SANGREMANO. I was at the federal prison at Estamos, California, when the incident of the birds occurred, serving three-to-five for computer service theft, first offense. This story has been told many times, mostly by people who were not there that day, or by people who have issues about corruption in the prison system or class politics being behind the war on drugs, and so on. The well-known Mr. William Hanover of the Aryan Brotherhood, he was there, and also the person we called Judy Hendrix; but they sold their stories, so there you're talking about what people want to buy.

I didn't leave that day, though I was one of Emory's men. Why I stayed behind is another story, but partly it is because I could not leave the refuge of my hatred, the anger I feel toward people who flick men like me away, a crumb off the table. Sometimes I am angry at people everywhere for their stupidity, for their buying into the American way, going after so many products, selfish goals, and made-up desires. Whatever it was, I stayed behind in my cell and watched the others go. The only obligation I really felt was to the Indian,

Emory Bear Hands. Wishako Taahne Tliskocho, that was his name, but everyone called him Emory, and he didn't mind. When I asked him once, he said that when he was born his fists came out looking like bears. He was in for theft, stealing salmon. Guys who knew the history of what had happened to the Indians thought that was good. They said it with a knowing touch of irony. Emory, he didn't see himself that way.

I was put in his cell block in 1997 when I went in, a bit of luck, but I want to say I was one of the ones who convinced him to hold the classes, to begin teaching about the animals. Emory told us people running the country didn't like wild animals. They believed they were always in the way and wanted them killed or put away in zoos, like they put the Indians away on reservations. If animals went on living in the countryside, Emory said, and had a right not to be disturbed, then that meant the land wouldn't be available to the mining companies and the timber companies. What they wanted, he said, was to get the logs and the ore out and then get the land going again as different kinds of parks, with lots of deer and Canada geese and lots of recreation, sport hunting, and boating.

I'd never heard anything like this, and in the beginning I didn't listen. Wild animals had nothing to do with my life. Animals were dying all over the place, sure, and for no good reason, but people were also dying the same. I was going with the people. Two things, though, started working on my mind. One time, Emory was speaking to a little group of five or six of us, explaining how animals forgive people. He said this was an amazing thing to him, that no matter how much killing and cruelty animals endured—all the songbirds kids shot, all their homes plowed up for spring planting, being run over by cars—they forgave us. In the early history of people, he said, everyone made mistakes with the animals. They took their fur for clothing, ate their flesh, used their skins to make shelters, used their bones for tools, but back then they didn't know to say any prayers of gratitude. Now people do—some of them. He said the animals even taught people how to talk, that they gave people language. I didn't follow that part of the story, but I was familiar with people making mistakes—animals getting killed in oil spills, say. And if you looked at it the way Emory did, also their land being taken away by development companies. It caught my interest that Emory believed animals still forgave people. That takes some kind of generosity. I'd wonder, when would such a thing ever end? Would the last animal, eating garbage and living on the last scrap of land, his mate dead, would he still forgive you?

The other thing that drew me in to Emory was what he said about totem animals. Every person, he told us, had an animal companion, a sort of guardian. Even if you never noticed it, the animal knew. Even when you're in prison, he said, an animal is on the outside living in the woods somewhere who knows about you, and who will answer your prayers and come to you in a dream. But you have to make yourself worthy, he said. You have to make a door in yourself where the animal can get through, and you have to make sure that when the animal comes inside that way, in a dream, he sees something that will make him want to come back. "He has to feel comfortable in there," Emory said.

Emory didn't say all this at once, like you'd read in a book, everything there on the page. If someone asked him a question, he'd try to answer. That's how it began, I think, before I got there, a few respectful questions. Emory conducted himself in such a way, even the guards showed him some respect. He wouldn't visit with the same people every day, and when guys tried to hang with him all the time, he discouraged it. Instead, he'd tell people to pass on to others some of the animal stories he was telling. When someone was getting out, he'd remind them to be sure to take the stories along.

The population at Estamos was changing in those days. It wasn't quite like the mix you see on the cop shows. Most everybody, of course, was from the street—L.A., Fresno, Oakland—and, yeah, lot of Chicanos, blacks, and Asians in for the first time on drug charges. And we had hard-core, violent people who were never going to change: some difficult to deal with, some of them insane, people who should have been in a hospital. The new element was people in for different kinds of electronic fraud, stock manipulations, hacking. Paper crime.

I divide this group into two types. One was people like me who believed the system was so corrupt they just wanted to jam it up, make it tear itself apart. I didn't care, for example, about selling what I got once I broke into Northrup's files. I just wanted to scare them. I wanted to hit them right in the face. The second group, I put them right in there with the child molesters, the Jeffrey Dahmers. Inside traders, savings and loan thieves who took money from people who had nothing, people who got together these dime-a-dozen dreams—Chivas Regal for lunch, you know, five cars, a condo in Florida. Every one of them I met was a coward, and the cons made their lives miserable. Of course, we didn't see many of these real money guys at Estamos.

We had gangs there, the Aryan Brotherhood, Crips, Dragons, Bloods, all the rest. These could be very influential people, but the paper and electronic criminals, the educated guys, almost all white, they passed on it. If one of these guys, though, was a certain type of individual to start with, he might help a gang member out. Even mean people. Even not your own race. Prepare their appeals, lead them through the different kinds of hell the legal system deals you.

Emory, who was about fifty, was a little bit like those guys. He spoke the same way to everyone, stayed to himself. Even some of the Aryan brothers would come around when he talked. The only unusual thing I noticed was a few of the more educated whites made a point of ignoring Emory. They'd deliberately not connect with him. But there were very few jokes. Emory was the closest thing to being a real spiritual person most of us had ever seen, and everybody knew, deep down, this was what was wrong with the whole country. Its spiritual life was gone.

When I first asked Emory about teaching he acted surprised, as though he thought the idea was strange, but he was just trying to be polite. My feeling was that by telling stories the way he could, he was giving people a way to deal with the numbness. And by identifying with these animal totems, people could imagine a way over the wall, a healing, a solid connection on the outside.

Emory declined. He said people had been telling these stories for thousands of years, and he was just passing them on, keeping them going. Some of the others, though, talked to him about it, kept bringing it up, and we got him to start telling us, one animal at a time, everything he had heard about that animal, say grizzly bears or moose or even yellow jackets. Some guys wanted to learn about animals Emory didn't know about, like hyenas or kangaroos. He said he could only talk about the ones he knew, so we learned about animals in northern Montana, where he grew up.

Emory spoke for about an hour every day. The guards weren't supposed to let this go on, an organized event like this, but they did. Emory would talk about different kinds of animals and how they were all related and what they did and where they came from—as Emory understood it. Emory got pretty sophisticated about this, and we had some laughs, too, even the guards. Sometimes Emory would imitate the way an animal behaved, and he'd have us pounding on the tables and crying with laughter watching while he waddled along like a porcupine or pounced on a mouse like a coyote. One time he told us there was so much he didn't know, but that he knew many of these things had been written down in books by white people, by people who had spoken to his ancestors or by people who had studied those animals. None of those books were in the prison library, but one of the guards had an outside library card and he started bringing the books in so Emory could study them.

For a couple of months, a long time, really, it went along like this. People wanted to tell their own stories in the beginning, about hunting deer or seeing a mountain lion once when they were camping. Emory would let them talk, but no one had the kind of knowledge he had, and that kind of story faded away. The warden knew what Emory was doing and he could have shut it right down, but sometimes they don't go by the book in prison, because nobody knows what reforms people. Sometimes an experiment like this works out, and the warden may get credit. So he left us alone, and once we knew he was going to leave Emory alone our wariness disappeared. We could pay attention without being afraid.

That tension came back only once, when Emory asked if he could have a medicine pipe sent in, if he could share the pipe around and make that part of the ceremony. No way, they said.

So Emory just talked.

Two interesting things were going on now. First, Emory had drawn our attention to animals most of us felt were not very important. He talked about salamanders and prairie dogs the same way he talked about wolverines and buffalo. So some guys started to identify with these animals, like garter snakes or wood rats, and not with wolves. That didn't make any difference to us now.

The second thing was that another layer of personality began to take hold on the cell block. Of the 120 of us, about sixty or sixty-five listened to Emory every day. We each had started to gravitate toward a different animal, all of them living in this place where Emory grew up in Montana. Even when we were locked up we had this sense of being a community, dependent on each other. Sometimes in our cells at night we would cry out in our dreams in those animal voices.

I identified with the striped skunk, an animal Emory said was slow to learn and given to fits of anger and very independent in its ways. It is a nocturnal creature, like me. When I began dreaming about the striped skunk, these dreams were unlike any I had had before. They were long and vivid. The voices were sometimes very clear. In most of these dreams, I would just follow the skunk, watching him do things. I'd always thought animals like this were all the time looking for food, but that's not what the skunk did. I remember one winter night in the dream I followed the skunk across hard-crusted snow and along a frozen creek to a place near a small treeless hill where he just sat and watched the stars for a long time. In another dream, I followed the skunk into a burrow where a female had a den with two other females. It was spring, and there were more than a dozen small skunks there in the burrow. The male skunk had brought two mice with him. I asked Emory about this, describing the traveling and everything. Yes, he said, that's what they did, and that's what the country he grew up in looked like.

After people started dreaming like this, about the animals that had chosen each of us (as we understood it now), our routine changed. All the maneuvering to hold positions of authority or safety on the cell block, the constant testing to see who was in control, who was the most dangerous, who had done the worst things, for many of us this was no longer important. We'd moved into another place.

Emory himself didn't make people nervous, but what was happening to the rest of us now did. The guards, just a little confused, tried to look tougher, figure it out. Anytime you break down the tension in prison, people can find themselves. The gangs on our block, except for the Aryan Brotherhood, had unraveled a little by this time. People were getting together in these other groups called "Horned Lark" and "Fox" and "Jackrabbit." Our daily schedule, of course, never changed—meals, lights out, showers—but all through it now was this thing that had gotten into us.

What was happening was, people weren't focused on the prison routine anymore, like the guards playing us off against each other, or driving each other's hatred up every day with stories about how we'd been set up, who was really to blame, how hard we were going to hit back one day. We had taken on other identities, and the guards couldn't get inside there. They began smacking people around for little things, stupid things. People like Judy Hendrix, who thrived on the sexual undercurrents and the brutality on our cell block, started getting violent with some of their clients. The Aryan brothers complained Emory had stirred up primitive feelings, "African feelings," they called them. Their righteousness and the frustration of the guards and the threat of serious disruption from people like Judy Hendrix all made Emory's situation precarious.

One day the story sessions just ended. They moved Emory to another cell block and then, we heard, to Marion in Illinois. With him gone, most of us fell back into the daily routine again, drifting through, trying to keep the boredom at bay. But you could hear those dream calls in the night still, and people told stories, and about a month after Emory left one of the guards smuggled the letter in from him that everybody has heard about, but which only Emory's people actually read. And then we destroyed it. He told us to hold onto our identities, to seek the counsel of our totem animals, to keep the stories going. We had started something and we had to finish it, he said. By the night of the full moon, June 20th, he wrote, each one of us had to choose some kind of bird—a sparrow, a thrush, a crow, a warbler—and on that night, wherever he was, Emory was going to pray each of us into those birds. We were going to become those birds. And they were going to fly away.

There were some who accepted right away that this was going to happen and others who were afraid. I would like to say that I was skeptical, but I was one of those who was afraid, a person for whom fear was the emotion on which everything else turned. I could not believe.

We got the letter on the 14th of June. The beatings from the guards, with people like Hanover and Judy Hendrix having a hand in it, none of that affected the hard-core believers, the guys they put in solitary. Especially not them. In solitary they'd turn themselves into the smallest birds, they said, and walk under the doors.

In that week after the letter came, a clear line began to divide us, the ones who were leaving, the ones who were going to stay.

The night of the 20th, about eight o'clock, sitting around in the TV room, I was trying to stay with a game show when a blackbird landed on the table. It cocked its head and looked around the way they do. Then I saw a small flock of birds like finches out in the corridor, swooping up and landing on the handrails on the second tier. A few seconds later the whole cell block was full of shouting and birdsong. The alarms started screaming and the guards stormed in. They beat us back into our cells, but by then birds were all over the place, flying up and down, calling out to the rest of us. My cellmate, Eddie Reethers, had told me he was going to be a wild pigeon, a rock dove, and it was a pigeon that hopped through the bars and flew past me to the window of the cell. He kept shifting on his feet and gazing down at me, and then he stepped through the bars out onto the ledge and flew away. I ran to see. In the clear air, with all that moonlight, I could see twenty or so birds flying around. I jumped back to the cell door. As many were flying through the corridor, in and out of the cells. The guards were swinging away at them, missing every time.

Five minutes and it was all over. They shut the alarms off. The guards stood around looking stupid. Seventy-eight of us were at the doors of our cells or squeezed up against the bars of the windows, watching the last few birds flying off in the moonlight, into the darkness.

In the letter, Emory told us the birds would fly to Montana, to the part of northern Montana along the Marias River where he grew up, and that each person would then become the animal that he had dreamed about. They would live there.

ROWING IN EDEN
Erik Anderson Reece

The hands had flown off the clock at the Hotel Eden
and above its blank face

a small wooden door opened in silence
to announce the eternal now

The concierge introduced himself as Pascal
"*The* Pascal" we asked

He shrugged and said "Here at the Hotel Eden
you are what you were before the *the*"

He rang for the bellhop whose pillbox cap read *Apollinaire*
"*The* Apollinaire" (we couldn't help asking)

He blew a soap bubble out the bell of his tiny clay pipe
and said "Every poem is the world in miniature"

Then he showed us to our room on the eighth floor
right between *lilas* and *pensee*

Outside the window a troupe of angels
was dancing *Swan Lake* atop a single obelisk

Below the belfry a cockatoo still held in its beak
the chord that once woke monks to their vespers

Apollinaire suspected the bird was an invention
of the well-dressed American poet

who sat each day in the French garden
writing obscure madrigals on paper wings

"He says we are all fictions
but that he believes in us anyway"

The day stretches out infinitely
At the Hotel Eden where the hour is always the same

even your mind can only imagine the present
"It is a great relief" I admitted

Apollinaire smiled around the stem of his pipe
and said "It pleases the Chinese poets especially"

From the balcony I gazed out across the blue gulf
A woman in a tiny white boat rowed alone

with the clock's missing hands
"She never stays long" explained Apollinaire

"I've heard she prefers the Hotel de l'Etoile
on the other side of the horizon

where even the starfish (those masters
of every element) dive down from the sky

to hear Orpheus tear his throat each night
with the song of his eternal longing"

IT GENERALLY LEADS
A SOLITARY LIFE
OR LIVES IN PAIRS
Rick Moody

We do not know precisely the rate of growth of the young

   in immature birds the neck is reddish brown

     Too soon marred are those so early made

A lot of hugging, holding hands sometimes. He always
   used to push the hair out of my face

      Both briskly preen their feathers

    I'm an insecure person

Dynamic gliding is used in particular by large sea birds

   All Americans are entitled to enjoy a private family life

With love's light wings did I o'er perch these walls

We were both aware of the volume and sometimes
I bit my hand—so that I wouldn't make any noise

The acoustic performances depend on various internal and external factors

The constant use of the beak inevitably causes wear and tear

please be my friend

The true thing is shading into the imagined thing, all right?

Many of the 30 or so gifts reflected his interests in history, antiques, cigars, and frogs

This is a matter of sex between consenting adults

For never was a story of more woe

The curious nuptial display of the Great Crested Grebe

The difference in quality between different territories
makes it more convenient for a female to choose an already
paired male

He needed to acknowledge that he *helped fuck up my life*

Harming him is the last thing in the world I want to do

The remedies for the irrational consumer onslaught of our society do exist

The sun for sorrow will not show his head

Classification of birds:

      pheasant, grouse, gull, loon, heron, coot, stork

You want me out of your life,
    I guess the signs have been made clear for a while

      We met, we wooed and made exchange of vow

    Flight is undulating and irregular

I didn't have any panties on. I'd probably be in a mental institute without it

      Young birds are paler in color

    I may be subject to the upbraidings of all
      who are now witnesses of the present solemn ceremony

And what I assume you shall assume.

The girl floats around in her nightgown.

C'mon, it's me

I intend to reclaim my family life for my family

she had complained that he was making no effort to get to know her

she wanted to have sexual intercourse with him at least once

Call me but love and I'll be new baptized

The nest is made in a hole, in rocks, or in a tree, often near water

what the meaning of the word 'is' is

Every day can't be sunshine

And I assure you this information will be kept strictly confidential

As soon as you sleep and renew yourself in sweet clothes

> I thought I fell in love with this person who I thought was
> such a good person

> A rose by any other name

Woman's body at auction

> It usually increases any feeling of awe or wonder
> that you've got going

> *Our position could not be more clearly stated*

> Nuptial activity demands high expenditure of energy.

> She told me I looked fat in the dress

The air sacs that form an extension of the lungs are present in certain reptiles.

> More love with a little bit of obsession

> I'm sorry to bother you with this

But definitely love.

THE BOX ARTIST
Joyce Carol Oates

UNTO EVERY ONE *that hath shall be given, and he shall have abundance: but from him that hath not shall be taken away even that which he hath.* So Jesus rebukes the Box Artist, who is not bold enough to seize his subject.

The Box Artist must constantly troll for happiness. La Puente. Cerritos. Olympic Boulevard. In this cruelly deprived Year of Our Lord 1935. This summer in which dried, cracked earth of the hue of baked blood is turning to dust, blown by a Santa Ana wind. Traveling the streets of Los Angeles anxious and yearning as any rejected lover. The Box Artist must seek his happiness *out there.* The Box Artist understands that happiness is chance, and always unmerited. The Box Artist understands *we must create the improbable circumstances of chance that the yet more improbable circumstances of happiness will be revealed to us.*

Cypress, Alvarado, Santa Clara. Westward, eastward. El Nido to the south, La Mirada to the east. To the west, the Pacific Ocean, which revulses me, for *its vastness cannot be fitted into any box.*

The Nickel & Dime Diner on El Centro Avenue. Amid boarded-up storefronts GOING OUT OF BUSINESS! BANKRUPTCY! MUST SELL ALL! A clatter of trolleys, automobiles, and trucks and the heat haze stirred by the wind into a glowing phosphorescence of dust and grit. At El Centro and Cupertino, a building marked the LOS ANGELES ORPHANS HOME SOCIETY. Weatherworn red brick set back in a large, mostly grassless lot surrounded by an eight-foot mesh-wire fence. What the eye first notices about this building is that there are few windows, especially on the uppermost third floor. These windows are tall and oddly narrow, like squinting eyes; on the first floor, the lower halves are crudely barred. Peeling white "colonial" trim, tarred roofs, rusted fire escapes, and at the rear amid sand and thorny weeds the rudiments of a "playground."

A more melancholy "playground" I have never seen and I swear that it was this playground that initially drew me, and not the possibilities of the orphans—for it is rare that the children are released from their work duties to "play"—and at the time of my first visit, in the late winter of 1934, the playground was deserted.

Only by chance, at another time, did certain possibilities suggest themselves.

In the Box Artist's life of anxiety, yearning and sudden unexpected happiness there are such moments. One must only seek them without ceasing—as Saint Theresa spoke of prayer without ceasing until prayer becomes the very soul, and the very soul, prayer. *It is as if the automobile makes this turn unbidden by me* onto an unpaved service road beyond the orphanage. Scrub palm trees, broom sage, and hardy purple-flowering thistles coated in dust like exotic works of art. A flock of sparrows scatters at my approach.

How many weeks it has been since I discovered the Los Angeles Orphans Home. How many weeks observing the orphan children from my automobile, hunched down beside the window in the passenger's seat. When moved to take photographs, carefully I ease open the door—carefully! The Box Artist is a master of precision. The Box Artist is a master of discretion. No one notices the Box Artist, for he is as near to invisible as any adult male, of indeterminate age and with no distinguishing physical characteristics (even my height and weight oscillate from day to day dependent upon temperature and barometric pressure), might be. My automobile attracts no suspicious eyes, for it is a battered 1928 Ford, its shiny black exterior and dashing chrome worn by sun, rain, wind, and wind-driven sand to this dull pewter-glow that is the very absence of color. *The Box Artist is but an eye, a pair of hands, a fierce and implacable will.*

You would identify the children of the Los Angeles Orphans Home as orphans, even from a distance, in their faded-blue clothing that fits them like smudged daubs of paint, with their worn shoes, their spindly limbs, and raw scrubbed faces, like the faces of wooden dolls with awkwardly fitted glassy-teary eyes. They are "children" in but a technical sense. Many of them are midget adults, with heads disproportionate to their thin bodies. Even the youngest are not "childish." Such terms—"children," "childish," "childlike"—apply solely to *wanted children.* There is a recognition of this fact, or complex of facts, in the slump of their heads and the sag of their shoulders and the limpness of their legs even when they are engaged, under no adult's supervision, in "play." (The playground is sand and concrete. A meager set of swings, only just two, the third having been broken for months; a tarnished slide; a wooden teeter-totter.) In the late morning and again in the late afternoon the orphans emerge from the rear slot of a door, trudging outside to blink in the mica-bright sunshine, dazed with exhaustion from their work duties (what these are, I can only guess, though a few of the younger and more hopeful run for a brief while and a few, always boys, as if recalling the bold maneuvers of children beyond the eight-foot mesh-wire fence, will push at one another and jostle for possession of a swing, a seat on the splintery teeter-totter.

Weeks, months. My photographs were few and infrequently inspired. Yet every time the orphans appeared, my heart leapt in hope. A scrim would be drawn, as in a film theater, and I stared, stared—but the one I sought wasn't among them. Until one afternoon, a hot Santa Ana wind blowing out of the Mojave Desert and my eyelashes gummed with dust, I saw, I suddenly see, the Blond Child. A girl orphan I have never seen before, yet recognize at once.

It is she. She is the one. The one the box awaits.

In the late summer of 1935. In the earthen-floored cellar of the bungalow on Sacramento Street, East Los Angeles. Thirty-two wooden boxes stacked neatly against the walls and in each of these boxes was a "capture"—a snapshot, a small artifact, a stuffed, lifelike little bird. To the neutral observer the works of the Box Artist would be indistinguishable from trash, but each of the boxes was, to the Box Artist, a testament to those minutes, hours, sometimes days in which the box was executed. Even the relatively uninspired boxes, and there were some of these, were triumphs of a kind; they represented, to the Box Artist, the solutions to specific problems. *The box is the affliction for which only the box is the cure.*

Yet each "capture" was solitary. Each of the boxes stood apart from the others, though they were crammed together in that dank, airless space.

The one the box awaits, at last. The Blond Child, a little girl of eight or nine, swinging on one of the swings. She is new to the orphanage; at least I have never seen her before. Already in her faded-blue uniform she resembles the others—except for the fierce radiance in her face, and the speed in her little body. How desperate, flying on the swing with its crude creaking chains and hard, splintery wooden seat; how defiant, kicking and bucking, her white-knuckled hands gripping the swing above her head and her thin arms stretched taut, like a bird's wings partly wrenched from its body. Both her knees are scraped and bruised. Her "dirty blond" hair is curly and snarled. Her eyes are intense, staring; her dazed soul shines through her waxy-pale skin. A beautiful child, though wounded somehow, damaged. *The sorrow in being born, without love.*

She is one of them, now. The orphans of the world. Waiting to be loved. Waiting to be taken—"adopted."

I think—*I will adopt her. I will claim her!*

I will make her hurt, mangled mouth smile.

But of course, being the Box Artist, I can only take the Blond Child's photograph. And that only in stealth, hoping I won't be detected.

My heavy black box camera is gritty with dust. It's an old camera; I am forever blowing dust off the lens, polishing it with my handkerchief. After a few minutes I become reckless and leave the protection of my automobile to squat in the dirt beside the mesh-wire fence, hoping to be hidden by tall weeds; aiming my camera with the assurance of a hunter as, oblivious of me, the Blond Child swings ever higher. Her hair is ringlets sparked with fire, her skin glints like mica, her eyes are ablaze like tiny blue jets of flame. As she swings, her skirt is bunched over her bruised knees, there's a glimpse of white beneath, much-laundered and frayed orphan's underwear it is, and her heels kick upward, reckless as a colt's. The Blond Child swings carelessly off-balance, veering crooked and nearly falling from her seat as if her secret wish is to fall and crack her head on the dirty concrete. *No! no!* I whisper to her. *Don't injure yourself; the world will shortly enough do that for you.* In the creaking swing beside the Blond Child another, quite ordinary girl is swinging, not boldly at all but in a lackluster manner; an older, slump-shouldered girl, one who has been waiting to be adopted for years and has all but given up hope. But the Blond Child is new to the orphanage. The Blond Child will never give up hope.

I promise. Someday. Something—maybe.

The Box Artist is the artist of desire. The tenderness of desire that can never be consummated.

The Box Artist plucks the child's flying image out of the air as you might pluck a feathery little bird out of the air, a canary or hummingbird, small enough to fit in your closed hand.

The heavy black box camera grows heated with the effort. The shutter snapping! The mysterious film within, wound past the lens, imprinted with the Blond Child who is oblivious of it. (And yet, afterward I will wonder: Was she aware of me, in fact? Crouched here behind the mesh-wire fence, in a patch of dusty weeds? Was she play-ing a game, as precocious girl-children do, watching the Box Artist through lowered eyelashes and giving no sign—except a sly little purs-ing of her lips?)

Until abruptly the children's "play" is over. In dispirited columns they shuffle back through the slot of a door. Someone must have called them, or a bell has rung. A matron in a dark coverall appears in the doorway, commanding the children to hurry. How strangely obe-dient they are, trooping back into the warehouse within, a house of unwanted wares; the emptying playground releases them without resistance. Yet, bravely, the Blond Child continues swinging, pretend-ing not to have heard the summons. She's flying, kicking, bucking, jets of blue flame leaping from her eyes, more recklessly than ever. The matron shouts at her what sounds like, "You! Get down." For another few seconds the Blond Child dares disobey, then she too gives in. Like a bird wounded in flight, she returns quickly to earth.

How forlorn, her abandoned swing.

The pathos of the *vertical, stilled* swing.

Indistinguishable now from the others—how many others, resigned, slump-headed in their faded-blue orphans' issue—the Blond Child disappears into the red-brick Los Angeles Orphans Home. My fingers continue to snap the camera's shutter as, after the death of its brain, a body may continue to thrash, to quiver, to pulse for a brief while. But at last I stop. Shaken and exhausted. My soul seems to have drained from me. Quickly, fumbling with my car keys, I prepare to leave; in a sudden terror that *the matron has seen me.* As in the past, not frequently but sometimes, occasionally, vigilant par-ties, invariably women, have called the police to report—What? Who? What crime have I committed, with only a camera? The Box Artist is bound by no local law in the execution of his exacting art.

As I drive away in the 1928 Ford I peer anxiously into the rearview mirror. Seeing only a dust tunnel raised in my wake.

My defense would be *The child knew me, as I knew her.*

>―›―◦―‹―≺

For hours that evening, and then for days. In the dank earthen-floored cellar of the bungalow on Sacramento Street, East Los Angeles. A shabby house surrounded by palm trees, crude sword-shaped leaves rustling in the ceaseless maddening wind. The whisperings and murmurings of strangers *Look! look! look! look! Look what his life is.*

Yet unhurried, I develop my film, precious to me as my very soul. My pulse quickens as I contemplate the miniature images, I feel almost faint, the Blond Child so captured, so *my own.* I prepare the Box; the Box I have chosen for her measures approximately thirteen inches by nine by five; an ordinary wooden box you would say, and you'd be correct; stained from use, oil smears in the wood slats; a box scavenged by the sharp-eyed Box Artist out of a mound of trash in a drainage ditch out behind this bungalow. Eagerly then, and in excitement and fear, I select my artifacts. In honor of the Blond Child I must choose well; if I fail, she will be lost a second time.

This is my body, and this is my blood. Take ye and eat. The secret wish of all who live in their art.

After several blunders, and sleepless nights, I step back to discover that I have created a Box landscape of uncanny subterranean beauty! Coarse, earthen, primitive; of the rich sepia hue of memory. Tiny snapshot-images of the Blond Child are secreted in the Box's dark corners and beneath a heart-shaped rock covered in dried dirt that I brought back from beside the mesh-wire fence. A vividly yellow bird, canary or goldfinch, purchased from the taxidermist from whom I purchase all my creature-artifacts, is placed on top of this rock, tiny talon-claws secured by glue to the rock. With tweezers I have managed to lift the little bird's wings from its body so that it appears about to fly away; its pert little tail feathers are at an upward angle that, too, suggests imminent flight; but never, never will the little yellow bird fly out of my Box, as the Blond Child will never fly out of my Box.

Of your fleeting and unloved life I make you immortal.
Of your broken heart, I make art.
Out of that lost day have I plucked you, and myself.
Yet, you are alone in the Box. I, doomed to invisibility, am
forbidden to take my place beside you.

SHOWING AN EPISODE

Diane Williams

Oh well, my life—or so I must have one—is very
crackalured and thin-shelled, encrusted with gold and
carved walnut on a moonlit evening, in the warm light,
as if in a lukewarm fire, where no actual cruelty
occurs. When I say which night, or the year this is,
or the name of my mother, I have more sympathy for her.

The strand of havoc-rendering beads Mr. Wang gave
to her hangs around her neck for what good that will do
her.

She is well-known and she lives in New York City.
It is well-known she is meant to be kept safe. She
bestows blessings and she will come easily to the lips.
In my life, she smiles.

I train myself to forget all that. I used to be
so worried. I think I have not been good enough yet.
You know the men I like won't fuck me.

I am now officially rippling, some of the time
optimistically, for I am a trained girl.

I forget to care about my leg, though.

"You go in there. Go in there." I go in there.
"In you go again. Do you have to sit in the—what is
the opposite of sun?" the mother says.

"Shade," I say.

"Shade," she says. "If you want to sit in the
shade, there are lots of places to sit. Do you like
it? You don't like it. It looks as if you don't like
it."

"I like it. What would we do?" I ask her.

"We will play and we will work."

"Will we fight?"

"Not very much."

"You know so much," I say, so next week I will do that. No, I won't. This is a very busy time for me. Perhaps after the new year. I kiss her lips.

What I have done is fabulous. I seem to be getting a little emotional. I keep pointing upstairs. I point upstairs again. I don't know if I will ever give a little chuckle. I plead in the corner. I was quite favored about a mile away from India. I asked Edward if he wanted more than anything not to be unkind to me, that was how coldly and calmly I was determined to be passionate.

THE CURSIVE EXAMPLE

Howard Norman

SINCE I COULDN'T SLEEP, I toured the farmhouse. There was little new in this. Tea would've been better, but I percolated coffee, then drank a cup, an accompaniment to being awake, not the cause. The night would be less wretched because I'd learned to consider insomnia an expertise. The farmhouse was built in 1847. I got up from bed; out the second-floor window there was a startlingly moonlit field. "Flooded." The crabapple tree could be seen almost in its entirety. My wife was asleep. My daughter was asleep in her bedroom, with its view of the barn awash in moonlight. I was wearing boxer shorts and a black T-shirt. It was a balmy summer night, 3:00 a.m. I had never kept a *Journal of Insomnia*. In this situation, my friend, DM, would have brewed tea. I felt like meeting DM in The Village Restaurant in Hardwick, but at this hour I couldn't by all etiquette telephone, though DM would've embraced the reason. Crickets were thrumming in the mudroom. Its broken ceiling, mouse entries, torn screen door made it "open to the elements," both an interior and exterior space. Like a Joseph Cornell *environment*. The inside crickets duet with the garden crickets faintly contributed to by the staccato hoots of a saw-whets owl. In the trees the owl's call was ventriloqual; I couldn't say exactly where the owl was located. A summer earlier I'd taken a night-long course, "Vermont Owls." I'd bought a new flashlight. One man had strips of glow-in-the-dark tape on each wrists. I couldn't figure out his need for these distinguishing marks. When it comes to coffee, I thought, "percolated" isn't a word much used these days. In the downstairs rooms, it occurred to me, on most every wall was a bird painting or print. In this respect, the house was like a historical aviary. The presence of these works was the result of the only form of acquisitiveness I was not ashamed of, except the beloved house itself. It was in 1973 that I purchased my first bird art, *Bengal Crow*, 1785, by Aert Schouman (1710-1792), at auction for $2,400. That sum comprised roughly one fifth of my income for the year. In 1979, I sold *Bengal Crow*, under sad duress, for $8,500 to the exact same person who'd auctioned it off in 1973. He had written to me, "I've thought from day one it was a mistake to ever let it go." I needed the money; I also acquiesced to his regret. Eventually, I used part of the money to pay rent, travel to the arctic, put a down payment on *Parrot*, by Edward Lear, to a private owner in San Francisco. Once you put your name out there, notices of bird art come in fairly often. In a 1984 catalogue from a famous auction house, I saw *Bengal Crow* again. On auction day I phoned in a bid, but *Bengal Crow* had been sold minutes before—it went for $13,000. I wondered if ill fate had befallen the seller, and, if so, what sort. I wondered if in years to come he'd write another letter.

━┥◆┝━O━┥◆┝━

One night, very late, reading *The Cryptogram*, a play by DM, in the guest room so as not to disturb my wife, I heard a car go past, "Duke of Earl" on its radio. The song drifting out. I wondered if the saw-whets owl heard it. The song brought back some memories, from even before it had been recorded. Like of my older brother's girlfriend, her name was Paris, who, in 1959 often wore a T-shirt that read EXIST TO

KISS YOU. She owned a pet parrot. My brother had fixed a hook to the ceiling of the car over the back seat of his 1948 Buick, so that Paris could hang up the parrot's cage while they were cruising around Grand Rapids, Michigan, a hell-hole. The parrot's name was Screwloose. The Buick, a black hippopotamus of a car, had the word *Turboglide* in beautiful, silver cursive letters flowing across the dashboard. Metal letters. The car had a gray plush interior, armrest ash trays, fuzzy dice hanging from the rearview mirror. I was having great, embarrassing difficulty learning to write cursive in elementary school. Paris suggested that I take a pen and paper, sit in the front seat, and, using the word *Turboglide* as a model, practice my handwriting. So I did that. (I would've done almost anything Paris suggested.) Whenever I saw the car in the driveway, I'd get my pad of paper, pen, and the two-page guide called, "The Cursive Example." My teacher used that phrase for our weekly handwriting assignment: "Time for our cursive example, students." One time I filled up a dozen or so pages, *Turboglide, Turboglide, Turboglide,* and so forth, right while my brother and Paris were making out in the back sear. Finally, I got an A minus on my next cursive example, improving up from a C minus. (In retrospect, I think this allowed me to think of the act of writing as having erotic possibilities.) In the rear-view mirror that warm evening, I saw that my brother and Paris had their shirts off.

><+>+○+<+>+<

On the wall next to the piano is *Head of a Flamingo*, by Mark Catesby. It was drawn circa 1740. Catesby did not, as Audubon did, only replicate what he saw in "the natural world." Catesby combined disparate elements into mesmerizing tableaux. He floated the flamingo's head, for example, in front of a branch of coral which normally be found underwater. In his bird drawings, Catesby offers an "ornithological expression," rather than merely an "ornithological experience." A very dear friend prefers to sit facing away from *Head of a Flamingo*, because, she says, "I invariably dream about it." I have two heroes: Mark Catesby and the Japanese writer Ryonosuke Akutagawa, who wrote *Hell Screen* and *Rashamon*, among other works. "What good is intelligence," Akutagawa asked, "if you can't discover a useful melancholy?" I often see Catesby's entire Natural History *oeuvre* as being underlit by a kind of melancholy, in that even bird art can be autobiographical in tone. Catesby, painter of birds, fish and flowers, never left a self-portrait. Testimony as to his demeanor is scarce. However, his friend, Emanuel Mendez de Costa, left a verbal sketch of Catesby: " . . . tall, meagre, hard favoured, and with a sullen look—extremely grave or sedate, and of a silent disposition; but when he contracted a friendship was communicative and affable." Catesby was also severely nearsighted.

Thomas Pynchon's novel, *Mason & Dixon*, deals head-on with the haunting levels of loneliness born of long years in the early American wilderness. One of the powerful aspects of this inimitable work, is that Pynchon engenders an empathetic loneliness of uncanny dimensions in readers—in me, at least. Of epic loneliness, historian D.L. LaPorte writes: "Mountain men are good examples, but there are other examples of commensurate import—long-time wilderness experience is what draws in eccentrics, and also creates eccentrics of a more extreme sort." I think that DM might agree that Jaime deAngulo would be one of those. Rogue ethnographer/linguist/poet, deAngulo lived in Northern California in the first half of the twentieth century. He spoke at least a dozen California Indian languages and all but invented anecdotal linguistics, that is, autobiographical linguistics. DM and I have exchanged books by deAngulo, and while I've never asked him outright what he thinks, I know he admires the writing, which is really all I need to know. On crows, deAngulo now and then offers a disquisition: " . . . well, first of all, they walk on two feet. You could see that as a mockery of humans. Also, crows could be considered the first linguists, at least in Northern California cosmology—they spoke every human and animal tongue, plus crow-talk, naturally, and they equally mocked all inarticulate gesture, whether in humans or animals, or themselves. I one said to Jung that crows were self-reflective. He didn't even feign the slightest interest." DM has a lovely pond out back on his property. Standing next to it after swimming in it one afternoon, I mentioned to DM that a neighbor was about to hire someone to shoot a great blue heron who, most every day that summer, arrived to her pond to eat frogs and fingerling trout. "It's eating all the fish," that neighbor said. I said that in my view her pond had been anointed. "She should provide for the Gods," said DM.

><>·O·<><

On the wall opposite a quilt that my wife made, is the Inuit print, *Laughing Gull*. The title is a literal interpretation of the action: the gull is indeed laughing. However, flying out of the gull's throat is a naked Inuit man, followed by items of clothing, such as mukluks, mittens, parka, and assorted spears, knives (*ulus*), dog sled reins, other implements of quotidian life in the arctic. *Laughing Gull* is composed in the simple, almost hieroglyphic manner of the earliest Inuit drawings allowed for public and commercial presentation, which would be roughly from the late 1940s or very early 1950s. In the autumn of 1977, I was living in the Beluga Motel in Churchill, Manitoba, a town located at the mouth of the Churchill River on Hudson's Bay. I was mainly engaged in translating stories about Noah's Ark as told by Mark Nuqac, an Inuit elder. One day, there was a break in the weather and I propped open a window using a Gideon Bible. I left the room to get breakfast at the Tundra Hotel and when I returned, a gull was perched atop my old Underwood typewriter. The gull had already unraveled the ribbon, was maniacally squalling, its muddy footprints all over the table. Later, I mentioned this to Mark Nuqac. "Any tracks on the floor?" he asked. None, I said. "It flew directly in through the window, eh?" he said. When I got close, the gull scattered out through the open door.

><>·O·<><

I was up at 5:00 a.m. reading DM's essays and recollections in *Writing In Restaurants*. It was just getting light out. I decided to drive over to the old waterwheel housing in Maple Corner. For a number of days I had been observing a kingfisher working the pond there. I took *Writing In Restaurants* along with me, thinking it might be nice to sit reading with my back against the weathered, splintery wood of the wheelhouse. It was about a ten minute drive to the wheelhouse. When I stepped from the car, I immediately glimpsed the kingfisher. It was on the telephone wire, then flew over to the roof of the wheelhouse, then flew back to the wire. "Kingfishers have punk haircuts," my daughter, Emma, had said. I was aware, in the early light and breeze off the pond, that if your criterion is succinct enough, moments of perfection might truly exist. Shorts, T-shirt, tennis shoes on, a book, a breeze off the pond, smell of old wood, a kingfisher plummeting along its sight line now and then, a world without humans except in a book—*happiness* was beside the point.

⋗—⊦◆⊷—○—⊶◆⊦—⋖

Screwloose ambushed silence, squawked and spoke in broken utterances as if attempting to translate the rain forest dialect in which he thought and dreamed into the 1950's English he eavesdropped on day after day, my brother speaking, Paris speaking, the car radio. Actually, the parrot's voice most closely mimicked that of the radio DJ, whose name was Ambroce Ambroce. Ambroce began his morning show with, "How ya doing this morning, my fine feathered friends?" Paris, at our breakfast table, would hear this, turn to Screwloose in his cage and say, "He's addressing you, sir. Be polite. Answer Ambroce Ambroce's question, you stupid bird!" One morning, I accidentally happened upon Paris naked from the waist up, standing next to the dryer in the basement. Through the oval glass, I could see her EXIST TO KISS YOU T-shirt tumbling. My mother was at work. My father was who-knew-where. My brother was working on his car. The hood was propped open. Naturally, I stared. Paris turned around. "Hey, there," she said.

"I got an A minus on my cursive example," I stammered.

"Well, that's very good," she said "But, hey, look. A girl needs her privacy."

When I went outside, I heard the parrot railing from the back seat, *"This is Ambroce—ka, ka, ka, Ambroce, reeeechak, reeeechak, don't ya know."*

— *for* DAVID MAMET

CONSTRUCTION
John Burghardt

wanted to make an end—because the end
was motion, nothing. He'd been leaving too, out of the nest
of tubing, little taped-up breathing egg. You'd watch his chest.
I'd watch you doze: the bars, your face, your breathing hand suspended
with the paper swans in the mobile—
but probably I dreamed that too. The air-
conditioner was a little monastery
plainsinging commercials.
                              "Coffee?"

                                        "Please."

                                                  I thought you'd feel
him moving in your hand. If I had gotten back
in time—or *in* time: in a poem, in the week
I walked these syllables across the lake, thinking my bleak
mood was just winter, even the lines I thought would carry going slack:
I kept saying them faster, trying to revive them. Breath
was feathering my fingers

BOXED IN

Paul West

FATHER GARNET SHRINKS from the renaissance outside his bolthole, not because he trickles and gurgles with sudden eruptive swaggers of his tripes, but because the huge polity out there bellows Death To Jesuits, as if any one label sufficed to evince this polymath, baritone singer, adroit mellow speaker, earthy Derbyshireman still close to the loam that bore him, his little knotted soul all chirps and cheeps, weary of going on being careful even as he reminds himself that memory is the pasture, the greensward, on which the mind can disport itself most ably, molding everything to the shape of heart's desire. On a sailor's grave, he recalls, no flowers bloom. He wonders where he heard that, and why, able here to summon all his mental *moutons* into one flock, baa-ing the gospel according to Saint Garnet, that not too gaudy, too precious, stone. Doomed to practice it day after day, even to the extent of dipping his nib in orange juice to make the words invisible, he has fallen in love with secrecy.

Once again he hears the noise of himself, squirreled away here in a priest hole made by a maimed dwarf of a carpenter who also

happens to be a lay brother. Saved by woodwork, and a little tamper-
ing with the original masonry, Garnet languishes in the bosom of a vast
country house—or rather in a thimble carved within a nipple—waiting
for daylight, unable even to stand in the space allotted him. Why, he
moans, are we hated so? He sneezes, once, twice, pressing his nose
hard to quell the seizure, each time murmuring the time-honored formula, Bless you, that saves the soul from being flung far away, angelic
silver skein aloft amid the tawdry of this world, never to return. You
could sneeze yourself soulless. But he never will, although strictly
speaking someone other than you should babble the housekeeping,
nose-saving formula. *Dieu vous aide,* he knows, is what the soul-
saving French neighbor says, automatic in this as in almost every other
prayer. It is good, he reassures himself, to be prayed for in this way by
just about anyone standing nearby. So, what does the King do when
he sneezes? Bless himself or have a chorus of courtiers mumble the
phrase? That is what they are there for, to keep his soul in his body in
the interests of, well, not the one and only church, but his sect anyway. Father Garnet thinks that for the soul to speak it should have a
language of its own, pure and godly, unknown to humankind and
therefore blessing itself in blindest esoterica. Now, there's just the
kind of phrase to get him damned, socially at least, hoicked out of his
hidey-hole and hanged along with hundreds of other mildly dissenting
churls. Father Garnet has no room in which to shrug, but his mind
makes the motion for him.

   This carpenter troubles him, this builder of hiding holes. He,
Garnet, prefers the old-fashioned country word *joiner.* Little John
Owen, the joiner in question, makes a fetish of joining priests to their
mouseholes, almost as if he thinks of the priesthood as a furtive, shy
calling: nothing of titles and fancy robes, but the essential spirit hidden
within the rind of the planet, within all these lavish country houses.
Hide-and-seek is not far from it, not when daily or even nightly life can
be shattered at any hour by the arrival of priest-hunting poursuivants
armed with torches and dogs, probes and huge cones of bark through
which they listen to the masonry, the chimneys, the passageways.

Garnet chides himself for thinking ill of his savior, but sticks to his point nonetheless: hiding us away as he does, and making endless provision for ever more of us all over the Midlands and the South, he presumes to some kind of power, making us invisible and yet at the same time even more spiritual than ever, more abstract, more distant, more creatures of the mind than of ritual, splendor, office.

It is like being made obsolete, he tells his creaking bones, remembering only too well the crippled joiner's instructions: "You will not stand, Father, you will have to contain yourself at the crouch, there can be little easing once you have been installed. To make your little place any bigger would be to expose you." He is a priest-shrinker, as alive in his trade as the old word for plough in such a word as *carucate*, which means as much land as you might reasonably plough in a year. In a way, Father Garnet broods in his cramp, our Little John is the ideal candidate for these cubbyholes, but he has no need, can go abroad as he pleases, more or less an upright dwarf, bubbling with good humor and perhaps more than a little amused by the spectacle of us all crouched until doomsday. He is almost a sexton of the living, omitting only to smooth the earth over us at the last and no doubt tempted sometimes to seal us in with trowel and mortar, which, if we do not burst out while the seals are still soft, encases us forever. Between cramp and suffocation, we have a poorer life than we envisioned, far from the august panoply of the high-ranking prelate. Father Garnet, the ranking Jesuit in England, tries to soothe his mind with his own name, derived from the word *pomegranate,* the color of whose pulp approximates the stone. No use. The sheer inappropriateness of light hidden under a bushel provokes him and makes his stomach queasy, a fate little eased by recourse to the drinking tube that enters his hideaway from behind the wardrobe outside. A small pan, a slight tilt to the feeder, and water can reach its priest: anything that will flow, soup or gruel, just to keep body attached to soul. Father Henry Garnet of Heanor, Derbyshire, thinks of himself as a light.

Now he is trying to work out which is better: being alone in the hole or having another priest for company: Father Oldcorne, as on other occasions, or Father Gerard, as on a few. There is certainly more talk, he decides, but of such an abortive, thwarted nature it were better to keep still. Perhaps the pallid patter of the inward voice consorts best with secret living on the run from King James's hunters. For those eligible to have women with them—if any—it might be better, he reckons: not so much cuddling as meeting head-on a different point of view; after all, those bearing within them the secretest hiding place might better adjust to circumstances and so cheer up anyone with them. A Jesuit, he tells himself, should be able to reason the pros and cons without too much trouble, but he finds his mind blocked, twisted, perversely longing for daylight, sleep, a reassuring companion voice. Instead, he hears the echo of a refrain voiced by Little John Owen:

> Him that can't stand it tight
> May never see the morrow's light.

Small consolation, that. Imagine, then, the confessional even smaller than usual, even for the recipient, with the confessee granted room to squirm about during the painful act. What then? Should the priest freeze in there, shocked by what he hears? Should he practice in the confessional for the hole or vice versa? Has either any bearing on the other?

If there is any moral to be drawn from recusants' experiences of being hidden, it is that it is better, if you intend to hide, not to do so on your own premises—or on those of anyone else. Best go to Saint Omer with Father Tesimond. Or, if that proves impossible, make sure you deal with a country house that has no servants in it and is not located in any of the English counties. It is not that Robert Wintour and Stephen Littleton on the run, camping out in barns, washhouses, seed stores, stables, and byres, were found by a drunken poacher, whom they had to gag and bind, but that in their next abode, Hagley, the country home of "Red Humphrey" Littleton in Worcestershire, they were exposed by a certain cook, Findwood, who wondered at the excessive amount of food being sent upstairs. That Findwood receives an annual pension for his good deed goes without saying. When the poursuivants arrive, Red Humphrey denies everything, after trying to block their entry. "This is our home, you shall not pass." Something Roman in his demeanor pleases him at this point. They come in anyway and receive the immediate cooperation of yet another servant, David Bate, who shows them the courtyard in which the conspirators have gone to ground.

Hindlip is not far away, readied like a fortress, although who is to guarantee the behavior of servants when they hear of John Findwood's pension, setting him up as an eternal spy before the word gets out about him grafting himself onto the domestic life of some country house in order to undo it, pay promised, no vengeance as yet visited upon him. His breed will prosper in these gruesome times, and the trade of household spy will establish itself among the poor, almost in itself a revenge calling.

Anne Vaux and Father Garnet, Anne and Henry as they are now just about calling each other, have exhausted all means of delay, even standing their horses in the fashion of a love-seat, he pointing northward, she pointing south, in fervid contemplation of each other, with no help from tradition or literature, but left to the meager resources of eye and hand to express what is forbidden. Now they change places, advancing not at all, but feeling heavy at the much shrunken extent of land between here and Hindlip, that labyrinth of lighthouses; almost, Henry Garnet thinks, like Sicily in little. When at last after much dawdling (which Henry Garnet in his original way calls prevarication) they arrive at the rear of the building, he dismounts on a patch of ice, unassisted by grooms, and immediately slips backward, gathers himself to surge forward, then loses his feet altogether and crashes to the ground, in one fall slamming his knee, outside left ankle, his right thumb and his head on the virtually invisible ice. It is a poor welcome, but he survives it, feeling shaken and shocked, a whole series of fresh pains and aches moving through his body, and in his hands a potent trembling. Anne is almost in tears at this last sight of him before the mansion gobbles him up for what? A month or more. Already Mary Wharmcliff, a scullery maid with child by her lover on a neighboring estate, Blackstone Grange, where she has walked to confront him, has returned with news that Sir Henry Bromley, a local justice of the peace, eldest son of Thomas Bromley, who conducted the trial of Mary Queen of Scots—a brash, invasive family—was already on his way from who knows where, intent on combing through Hindlip from top to bottom. This leads, of course, to a further piece of wisdom that says: If you wish to move from one country house to another, say from Coughton to Hindlip, do not do it on horseback or by any other means that entails travel between two points, lest you gallop right into the gang led by one of the Bromleys. Nor, knowing this and some of the Bromley history, should you extend too much trust to the idea that Sir Henry, related to the recusant Littletons, might go easy on certain Catholics. The schizophrenia of the times allows him to do his job without, in this case, altogether losing face with Muriel Littleton, his sister. It is simply another variant of the William Byrd philosophy, enabling the happy practitioner to face both ways without ever being damned as a hypocrite. It is almost as if opinions, tenets, beliefs, were so many silken handkerchiefs to be floated about in the wind, no more committing you to a certain code of conduct than the passage overhead of a moulting sparrow. Whence, Anne Vaux asks herself, this new breed of trimmers, people who out of corrupt self-interest trim their conduct for each situation? Is this the fabled opportunism of wolves, or what Henry Garnet, rarely at a loss for a classical exemplum, calls *homo homini lupus:* man a wolf to man. Perhaps, though, she thinks, if nobody believes in anything very much then all persecution is going to come to an end, because nobody believes much in that either, except as entertainment for the mob. It is all too much for her, being severed here and now as Henry Garnet, with no time for a meal or a drink, goes his way to join those already cached in the house: The house chaplain, Father Oldcorne, and the lay brother Ralph Ashley. Outside, by special dispensation granted to himself, Little John Owen hides in a dwarf-adapted birdhouse that, through a miracle of hydraulics known to him alone, floats in a duck pond. Or it did; thanks to the freeze, it now sits there, compelling upon him all kinds of privation but permitting him, as he so often said during the design phase, fresh air galore. Crouched out there, the engineer and artificer of the whole hideaway (there is room for a dozen more, should need arise), he fulfils yet another part of his destiny, as much in charge of his scheme as Cecil of his, and indeed a consummate piece of the drama. Simply, as he designed it, the birdhouse goes over him like a cloak; he then steps into a specially designed circular punt, fashioned after the coracle, and waits, lowering the birdhouse to the coracle rim, which it exactly matches. Supplies abound, more or less, as if he is truly a flightless bird; the birdhouse is not round, but has a round base, and this, he has assured the Habingtons, aghast at his perverse ingenuity, enables the birdhouse to move around in the water, making it the center of a perfectly self-controlling motion. It spins itself very slowly, without favoring any particular direction, whereas a rectangular punt will not. As if itinerant birds have left emergency packages for later comers (the code of the distant, romantic log cabin in America), the Owen birdhouse contains in tiny compartments bits of twig, called locally Spanish juice, an import like strawberries, from Aranjuez; hazelnuts, beech nuts and roasting chestnuts; tiny pastry pockets of quince jelly; sunflower seeds collected in small leather pouches that might once have held rings; unicorns made of gingerbread, none more than two inches high. On the quiet, in the hours that are left over when he subtracts his work from his life, he bakes and rolls, stamps out two-dimensional pastries, and polishes nuts for storage. A squirrel, in short, with a higher destiny ever awaiting him: There will never, what with the new influx of priests from the Continent, be enough hiding places. Yes, he grins, chilled in his private minaret, you can't always get a good hiding even though you deserve one. Such wit warms him when nothing else does. Attracted by the small holes de rigueur in a birdhouse, some nonmigrating birds have already called on him, and he has made the reckless error of sharing his supplies with them, in the interior dark proffering what he can, a sunflower seed, say, between finger and thumb, with aviary refinement. Surely, he thinks, hardly giving a thought to Hindlip's crew of festive, garrulous servants, they will never find me here; I am too blatant. No, the birdhouse is. They will search the house, but nothing else save the outhouses and barns. This is much better than suicide with beautifully crafted swords or being shot in a courtyard or blown up by gunpowder arranged to dry out in front of a roaring fire like a drenched cat. When they come, they will bounce off, as always; I wonder why they bother. Well, it must be to earn their wages, little realizing their real wages will be paid after death, in another world altogether.

Put out by having to share a space with Father Oldcorne (this the safest in the entire house, Habington says), Father Garnet tries to collect his wits, damaged by the fall on the ice. He feels hollow and brittle, crouched in a space he cannot stand in or stretch out in: almost a torture in its own right, inflicted by friends. He tries to fix his mind on some old Roman words, first discovered in childhood and treasured as jewels, but they will not come as once they did, when he was in a better mood or circumstances were less drear. It is as if the shock of falling on the ice, as well as making his head ache and feel sore to the touch at one point in his left temple, and upsetting his stomach too, has wiped out his memory, at least the verbal one. Come back, he says, trying an old trick to bring something to mind, catching himself in the act of naming it before he even tries to retrieve it. But only *tuli, latum,* come, and they in severed, broken form. He is not that much of an old Roman after all, he decides; all it takes to rattle him is a patch of ice and a household in a hurry. If he weren't who and what he is he would be inclined to say damn them all, but he refrains, wishing instead he could have an accompaniment from Byrd, of Byrd's music performed by any of them, himself included, but there is so little time. Byrd, he notes drily, feels no need to hide; why does he not happen to be on the poursuivants' list of undesirables?

Making matters worse, even as he poises on the brink of darkness at noon, there is the standard cooking smell of Hindlip, the savory aroma of beef and gravy familiar from his childhood, when he lurked by the big kitchen table with his sisters and they sampled various tidbits of the meal. A small spoonful of gravy would set him up, or, better, a square of Yorkshire pudding, crispy brown on the outside, soft yellow within, a substance designed to replace meat when meat is hard to come by. None of that, though surely it might have been prepared. A hot cup of almost anything would serve, he thinks; it does not have to have much taste, only be hot, so that the warmth will linger after he has descended into the hole. He gives up, still wrinkling his nostrils at the cooking smell, almost as if he could eat with them. It is later than lunchtime, but who is watching the time? The absent sun is no guide—only his aching, volcanic stomach. No small ceremony, then, with a few chaste words in any language softening the bleakness of the moment, as language, the dominator, mostly does, converting the worst of situations into an interpreted something. In an ideal world, "real" in the sense that Anne Vaux uses the word, he would be escorted (he loves the dignity and finesse of that word) upstairs to a small quiet room with clean sheets, there to sleep off the impact and stretch out his testy body. A pitcher of hot water would be there when he woke, and sundry other helps; a snack from the kitchen would set him to rights—it would not even have to be Yorkshire pudding or, if later, a wondrous trifle with custard and cream, peeled almonds, and sponge cake or gingerbread drenched in fortified wine. No such perfection needed, neither ambrosia nor ichor. He is willing to go dry, he tells himself; it is a mark of his courage, as one going to punishment, which is bound to come later—Fathers Gerard and Briant have already been through that particular honor. If only, throughout this process, he could sagely sleep, putting his feet where directed, scooping himself up with the expended smile of a man shoved past his limit.

What he does feel, rather than witness, is a host of hands nudging and easing him, pressing him this way and that, raising and lowering, prodding him to buckle left or right, palming his head forward as if it stuck out too far, and with gentlest toe tip of their own urging his feet to tuck themselves in better or he will never get all of himself into place. He nearly chokes, being adjusted into so strait a place, but he lifts the top of the moment off, as if dealing with boiled milk, tossing away the skin that says he might better have been naked for this, and oiled even, converted into a performing animal for the sake of safety. With muscles only a little more willing than not, he inches his way into the already established, pungent gloom that clings to Father Oldcorne, always a man of no great conversation, who twists and hunches as best he can while another human pushes into his space. The special aroma of the cancer-ridden Father Oldcorne is familiar to him; perhaps it is the bouquet of the self-flogger, the man who punishes his tongue as if it were some live, lascivious beast, corrupted by language. Father Oldcorne smells of burned leather, he decides—at least in close quarters he does—but this might be an effect of brief confinement; the smell is more that of rotting cauliflower, not a human aroma at all but direct from the kitchen's anteroom, where discarded celeries and crozzled leftovers are put, often tempting a mouse into the open. Father Oldcorne is not his choice of traveling companion, or even for sitting still with through the dismal watches of the priestly night; the man's hangdog, punished look, not visible in here, thank Jesus, puts him off, as does his constant need for praise for having subjugated his body to a greater degree than Garnet and Garnet's free-flowing, almost flamboyant friends. Oldcorne has a dun, grievous quality that restores those who have overlooked it to the miserable side of life; no one, listening to him or inhaling him, will want to live too long.

Much of this Anne knows, can divine from what Henry Garnet fails to say as he vanishes bit by bit into the architectural trap devised by Little John Owen who, thanks to the emergency of Sir Henry Bromley's squad impending, freezes out in the martin-house stuck in pond ice. Anyone finding him will turn into a purple martin. One hug and Henry Garnet is gone. She wonders how many hugs there have been: two or three, this by far the most final, seeing that once again they are gambling with their own lives and those of priests, actually standing here to marvel at the completeness of the disappearance when the hiding place should have been sealed off, the upstairs water tank shoved back into place by eleven pairs of hands. With so many in league, she thinks, how keep a secret as bizarre as this? Only in a recusant household habituated to such scenes can you get away with it. Perhaps we will. It is assuredly one of John Owen's most decisive inventions, with the one priest's toes beside the other priest's head, for hygiene's sake. She scoffs at the very thought of hygiene, knowing they had better hygiene in the Ark, and this is a Greek word come down from a people who, professing it, loved the word because they achieved nothing of the kind. The voice of Father Oldcorne, rattled, comes from behind the tank, which actually seems to amplify any sound they make. "A devil in hell," he is saying, always partial to the extreme view of things. Not a sound from Henry Garnet, who has never felt more like a parcel of dirty clothes stuffed into a moldy drawer by a feckless washerwoman. Henry Garnet has never made a fetish of answering Father Oldcorne, whose self-directed rhetoric implies the coldest reaches of the universe, the most fearful moments of any human life. He is not exactly a misery, but one who exaggerates, Henry thinks, the dark side of the human antic. Well, when he gets out of here in a month's time, he will have cause for complaint. No, not a month, a week will do; even less, once Sir Henry Somebody has performed his sullen chase through the enormous house and gone his truculent way, his commission from the Privy council fluttering in his hand. Father Garnet does not know that the Bromley team has been promised "a bountiful reward" for its best efforts, so that when they come they will screw their gimlets into the elegantly paneled walls with avaricious zeal—wherever a priest may be hovering (a favored word of the Privy Council, whose notion of priests involves a paradoxical angelic component that makes their lives difficult until they manage to combine angel with harpy). Everyone at Hindlip is familiar with the sounds of probing as, once again, the poursuivants, some recruited only for the day, sedulously go about the business of ruining good panel work, much to the distress of Maestro Owen. Such grinding and scraping suggests a house full of rats, which in a sense it is whenever these busybodies show up. Mostly from hovels themselves, they delight in the spoliation of luxury, delighted to bore holes in the eyes of the faces in portraits (who would hide behind *them?*) or next to an old borehole so that the two, plus another on another occasion, will form a peephole. By now, the house has a much-penetrated look, as if musketry practice of the wildest abandon has taken place in the dining room, the bedrooms, even lofts and closets. Father Garnet thinks of Hindlip as the *punctured house*, practiced upon by dunce doctors trying to let the blood out of it to no purpose—nobody has ever been found here, never mind how vehement and specific the official proclamation borne in the hand of the poursuivant who leads. John Owen is far too clever for them, and Hindlip gives him more scope than almost any other country house. They might as well look for actual faces in the coats of arms proudly displayed on the walls.

Anne Vaux knows she cannot stand any more of this, so she goes downstairs, unable to believe she has just ridden cross-country to entomb the dearest priest in the world. She has not so much participated as lent an ear, an eye, a heart. Now her stomach, always upset by riding sidesaddle—or any saddle—begins to come back to normal, less afflicted by the devious fragility of her robust-looking life. She is not that strong, she knows, what with eyes, womb, and—no, there is nothing else save the acid swilling about in her stomach. Not because she wants it, but because she associates it with conventional everyday conduct, she asks for an unusual lunch: ham and eggs, a dish often favored at Hindlip because the makings are always fresh. Gradually, overpowering the reek of cauliflower and the bouquet of roast beef, the companionable wideawake aroma of ham and eggs bubbling in hot lard ascends the stairs and seeps through the structure, reaching Henry Garnet and actually bringing a tear to his eye; why, this is the most exquisite torture, he feels, and surely Anne could stop it. Who on earth—no, he stops. It is no use getting into a swivet about a wrongly timed breakfast he would give his folding leather altar to devour. The smell will endure for at least a day; no windows open in November, and over the decades the house has brilliantly captured and fused its own smells, like a prisoner inhaling himself, until there is always a fused aroma—faint corky oversweet strawberry infused with an acrid spume of boiling vinegar—that serves as background to the smells of the moment. Against both delight and abomination, Henry Garnet decides to hold his breath, but he can do so only in upsetting spasms, and he soon gives up, at once rhapsodic and revulsed.

Anyone with a developed sense of coincidence, such as may be acquired after reading a great deal of Dickens, will wish Father Garnet never to have arrived, but instead to remain circling with Anne Vaux in some nondescript, drab field until the end of time. By the same token, one does not want to have Sir Henry Bromley arriving within half an hour of Garnet's reaching Hindlip. As zealots go, Bromley is fairly civilized, although his arrival coincides also with break of day; Henry Garnet's feeling that it is dinner time shows how exercised his mind has become (he's being previous as almost never), but Anne Vaux's craving for the ritual of ham and eggs reveals her attunement to a daily round, a regimen that both pleases and steadies. Amid the panic of their confusion, no one is saluting the dawn except the kitchen staff, who time their work by daylight and need only to be consulted once about, well, not so much time as the phase of the day. Sir Henry Bromley is too eager, having risen well before four in the morning to get his posse on the road.

So here they are, a motley team, some adorned in butcher's smocks with big tool pouches in front containing awls and spikes, boring-tools of all kinds, and little listening tubes with funnel ends. Some of them have teak mallets with which to tap on hollow-looking panels. They also have with them kindling to test the chimneys with, knowing full well that a lit fire in a fake chimney soon proves the case. Hargreaves is among them, but dragging a leg—he too from a fall on ice—but this time he kowtows to Sir Henry, who can make or break him depending on the skill with which he exposes the priests. They do not even recall who tipped them off about priests at Hindlip, but the word is out; perhaps it has always been out inasmuch as there has almost never been a time when priests were not at Hindlip. The

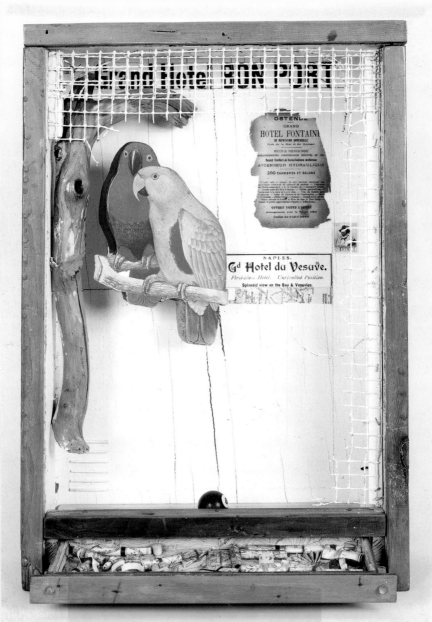

rumor and the event match each other, but to no advantage for the poursuivants, who have found no one at all during their previous searches. As it happens, Thomas Habington is not at home when the inquisitorial rabble arrive at the main door, but his return prompts some lively exchanges between him and Bromley.

"Do not brandish your proclamation, man," he bellows at Bromley. He speaks as a man who has already been in the Tower once. "I take your word for it. I will gladly die at my own front gate if you find any priests in here. Lurking under my roof! You will as soon find fish folded in among the tablecloths. We are who we are, Sir Henry." His vehemence cuts no ice; Bromley has seen it all before, the bluster and the indignation—he would cavort in the same fashion if he *were* hiding Jesuits. It goes with the suit, and Habington is not a "bad" man, just a misguided rebel with a taste for punishment: hence his impassioned cry about dying at his front door. There is no need for emotion, Bromley knows; either the priests are here or they are not, and he does not intend to go until the house has been ransacked, and indeed made to pay. It will take three days, he estimates, with his men rampaging around upstairs and downstairs, ignoring the protests of the Habington family and enigmatic visitors such as Mrs. Perkins, whom he has met before. The grinding, drilling, boring, go on all day, with naps taken in the big public rooms, nothing provided by way of food, but the kitchen raided until the staff feel demented, unable to function according to the strict rules of the house. That they mean to spend the night appalls Anne Vaux, who detects in their behavior a new resolve: Gone are the days of the lazy, casual, gentlemanly search; this is the work of plebeians eager for profit, and she works on her disdain, doing her best with stare and sniff to embarrass those who seem intent on taking the house apart.

"I actually turned people away," Habington is telling them; then, as he thinks better of it (priests, plotters; who else?) adds, "old friends who wanted to stay the night. I have a wife with child; I am far too busy for visitors. That includes you all."

"Quite so," Bromley says, himself doing nothing in the way of search; his servants do that for him. "I am not accusing you of being inhospitable, sir, or of uxorial coarseness. Oh no. I await only the conclusion of this business and will be happy to acquit you of any charges if we find nothing amiss. We have to be thorough, though, as your pig-scraper does, and your steeplejack. We cannot afford to skimp matters, sir. The national safety is at stake. As my father always said—"

But no one listens; he has been here before, with the same quotations, although a smaller crew. They intend to spend the night, sprawled anywhere soft, belching and grunting, drinking and quarreling, seeking the temporary oblivion the laborer needs from his hire. At such a time, Anne thinks, we might actually let the priests out, for a stretch and a snack, but there are so many of them you are bound to make a mistake. Little does she know it, but Bromley, an organized mind in an untidy life, has insisted that at least one man remain on guard on each floor, although how far any watchman can be trusted not to fall asleep he cannot know. If the priests make a move, he knows it will be by night. He resolves to stay awake until dawn, but realizes he has been on the go since today's, and readily exempts himself. Does he hope to find a priest or merely to achieve the most thorough fruitless search in the world? This Habington, he muses, is a rather rash person, but manly in bearing and, if a liar, one with plausible good manners. My sister lies in the same fashion. Yet I do not worry about her; her lies are between her and God Almighty. Some of us with the highest power blow both ways. We are not without sympathy, but work is work is duty. Will I ever have to rope my sister in, merely for being a Catholic? Never, so what's all the fuss about? If you strip away the varnish of religion, life is the same for all of us. If I were God, would I want to be prayed to? No, I would want to be left alone, lost in the lap of memory.

Even on the first day, through diligence and willingness to deface the house's interior, the poursuivants have found grist for their mill: three simulated chimneys with planks soot-blackened to resemble bricks, and cavities—chambers—full of trinkets and trumpery (as they say) ranging from books to rosaries, vases, chalices, and huge thick candles. "I am a collector," Habington raves, "I am entitled to put my things where I want. Nothing *has* to be on view." What, then, are these? They produce the title deeds concerning the estate, opening them up and riffling the pages amid their pink ribbons. "Are you telling me," he insists, "I have no right to put important papers in a safe place? Don't *you*? What does this signify? I am a landowner; I do not want people wiping their boots on legal papers or peering at them to see how much I am worth." Then they inform him that in the brickwork of the gallery surmounting the gate they have found two spaces, each large enough for a man. Why so many open cubbyholes? He tells them, in his protracted huff, that all country houses have such facilities, to store unwanted books, vases, hunting boots—"You know, Sir Henry," he says, with his most produced voice, coming on strong, "the sorts of things you don't want to part with but cannot stand to have under your feet. Any woman will tell you that. After all, dear sir, you found nobody in these places. There is nobody, as I said. I dare say, if you and the loyal Hargreaves wish to stay the night, as all the signs indicate, we can surely find so-called priest holes for you, in which you will feel so uncomfortable that you will just as soon recognize that they were never intended for human occupation. They are for storage, but you are welcome to try. A severe lesson cannot be more certainly learned."

"I respect our armor, sir," Bromley tells him, "but you must understand we will be here as long as necessary. Hargreaves will keep an eye on the house all night."

"No, Sir Henry, *I* will."

"No need, sir. Take your rest. I will take mine."

"Not in a priest hole, then. We do have rooms adjudged suitable for a gentleman."

"A sit-up sleep," Sir Henry tells him. "Taught me by my father." He is still pondering Habington's riposte about a country house's being so vast that you forget what you have and do not memorize a house by its cavities, whatever their purpose might be.

So: Anne Vaux ordered and got her ham and eggs just in time and so feels nourished for a fray in which she plays little part, now thinking of herself as merely a mouth, a tongue, likely to give evidence by accident. She keeps quiet, out of the way, wondering if music by Byrd might serve to lull the searchers, making them skimp and miss. Little John Owen, still out in the birdhouse in the pond, has done good work here, although perhaps these are not the best of his optical illusions. In one recently modified house he created a painting of a door opening on another door, three-dimensional until you get up close—just the sort of thing to suck in and confound a Hargreaves—but he has not done this everywhere. Another lifetime would help, she thinks. If only he had started work ten years earlier. Off she treads, out of the house, chunk of suet in hand to fasten to the side of the birdhouse in which he roosts—the side facing away from the house. It will be better than nothing, whereas cheese would alert their suspicions. All John Owen has to do is somehow help himself and try to keep the suet down. It is like wartime here, she decides, with troops garrisoned all over the privacy of the house. Is this how they treat the Jews in Europe? I am better doing this by day, in the open; they would wonder why I was doing it at night. If they keep watch, and they will. If Henry Garnet, who hurt his knee, cannot stand being cooped up, what are we to do?

In the blistering, gusty cold of that night, Wednesday leaking into Thursday, John Owen, who has been outside since Monday, cranks his almost petrified broken body out of the birdhouse, lifting it up and off him, and creeps into Hindlip through an entrance only he knows, thence into a hiding place known to most of them as Curly, because it does not lie straight and whoever is in it—in this case the lay brother Ralph Ashley, also there since Monday—can only lie curved. There is little room for two, but they wordlessly share the apple Ralph Ashley has been saving for three days. It is as cold in the house as it is outside, and Little John feels he has exchanged life for death. Ashley's body gives off no warmth. What they do next is rash, but they both feel dizzy, weak, can hardly move their legs; indeed, Little John is lucky to have stumbled in unseen. The kitchen tempts, the open road next. As Little John sees it, he is bound to be discovered if the searchers occupy the house long enough, and if he stays any longer in the birdhouse he will die of exposure. Wordlessly, they decide to move out, through the wainscot into a gallery. The house is still and only faintly lit. If someone catches them, they will give themselves up; perhaps the poursuivants will be satisfied with them, mistaken as to who they are. Out they slip, one foot caressing the other before going farther, but the house becomes an uproar; Hargreaves, on his third patrol of the night, wandering into the gallery out of boredom and with no expectations at all, catches sight of two shady figures tiptoeing their way into the hall and communicating with each other in dumb show. In a second, they have been surrounded and pinioned while Sir Henry, half asleep and blustering to compensate for his bleariness, asks them who they are. Just servants, they answer, unable to sleep. But sleepless servants, Sir Henry comments with a sniffle, do not wander through the main house at night like invited guests. Who are you? Are you Tesimond and Oldcorne, Greenway and Hall? He is wide of the mark, of course, but he is convinced he has caught someone, not of high station (he knows the smell of a servant when he sniffs one, and the whiff coming off them is quite different). Rather than interrogate them, he sends them off to his headquarters and occupies himself with the expectant mother, Mary Habington, sister to Monteagle, the savior of the hour.

"No fear, Sir Henry," she shrills, "not unless you carry me out yourself. I am staying here, where I belong. How dare you?"

Clearly he has no business trying to lug around someone so well-born and well-connected; he makes no offer to remove Anne Vaux, whose sharpened glare upsets him, so he retires again and writes a report to Cecil, waffling away about the devious ways of Catholics, hosts, country gentlemen, ladies of the house, and just about everybody not on his side. He will not sleep this night, nor will he hit on the truth, he is so eager to present himself in a good light as the finder, the exposer. Restrained enough in speech, he tends to hyperbole at the merest touch of self-esteem, informing Cecil that "of all the various scheming and truculent priests, those Jesu-wits, I have two of the vilest in hand, for prompt sending to you, sir, and your diligent punitations. I have one or two misgivings about who these people are, for they will not say, but truth told they have, without any airs or graces as of high-born gentlemen, that bloated humbleness we all recognize as bombast in reverse. We, who have not been educated for nothing, need yield no quarter to the Roman-suckled rabble of high priests. At your service always, with intaminate pride." He can go on in this vein for hours, sufficiently launched with writing materials, like someone taking to water for the first time and hitting on the correct stroke, even were he swimming in pitch. He calls off the search, explores his conscience, wishes he had not been so swift in sending them up to London, then renews the ransacking of the house into Friday, Saturday and Sunday, deeply conscious of interrupting a religious timetable that no one dares mention. From memory, in her diary, Anne Vaux writes as follows:

> We have here again, for the seventh day, the same behaviours as before at Baddesley-Clinton, which I fiercely complained of, though this house be none of mine and therefore not a subject for mine own remonstrances. Suffice to say, these poursuivants behave like a pack of bad boys playing blindman's buff, who in their wild rush bang into tables and chairs and walls and yet have not the slightest suspicion that their playfellows, God save them, are right on top of them and almost touching them.

She reads this through, crosses it all out as dangerous, then tears it loose, looking exasperatedly at the diary, flicks through some pages, wraps the volume in a fold of wallpaper she picks from a minty-smelling closet, and bears the whole thing downstairs to the roaring fire, into which she sets her life: unseen in the whole endeavor, for one glimpse of her ferrying something perilous to read would have them snapping at her heels. She realizes she is not living prudently: The constant hammering has unnerved her, given her a headache that reaches down the back of her neck into her shoulders, and the egg-and-ham breakfast is sitting none too well—days old, it seems to lie there and haunt her still, and she now agonizes at having put Fathers Garnet and Oldcorne through the miseries of its aroma. Indeed, nothing she does helps them. They are not in the lower chamber that sits below the dining room, where it would be possible to pass food down to them, as if they were plaintive dogs behaving well at their masters' feet. They do not even have an apple between them. She stews about Little John and Ralph Ashley, seized and sent away incognito, and knows there has come an end to hideaway-building. Further torture inflicted on John Owen will kill him certainly, and the whole recusant scheme will perish. It would be one thing if the searchers, having found the two, had gone, satisfied with their prey; but here they are still, racketing about, so much so that she twitches at every tap or rattle, every creak of the house as it settles down into winter repose. She recalls having noticed in herself and others a curious habit of completing a watched motion: when someone, bracing to move an arm or a leg, curtails the movement and the intent watcher goes through with it, for the moment identified into union with the person watched. This is how she feels about the two priests in their hole, sensing all the movements they dare not make and accomplishing them by guess-work. Will it always be thus? No, she knows, it is going to be much worse. The poursuivants, having found two, want to have two more, yelping and scattering, heedless of a house routine destroyed. Brave Mary Habington has refused to leave, but she finds their presence vile in the extreme, and all she can do is maintain a cool austere demeanor while her husband orates incessantly about an Englishman's home being his castle. Was he the originator of that saw? Well, castle no more, my loves, the rabble has entered its final playground and will not be contained by any code of decent manners. Sir Henry is already at odds with himself, she notes, for having not interrogated Owen and Ashley himself; whatever they said would be gold.

"The trouble is, my lady," Sir Henry is saying to her, "the moiety of this rabble we have here has not enough proper English to get someone to draw down their trews for the jakes, if you will pardon the reference. I am among apes."

"We are both, *all*, among apes, sir."

"Hence the high degree of choler among us."

He needs no spoken agreement, she can see that; he is accustomed to silent assent while he roams in hit-or-miss meditation, hoping for a coup that will raise him even higher in Cecil's esteem. In truth he finds Worcester a bore and would love to move to London, at an advantage of course. In Worcester jail at this very moment, to save his life or at least delay his execution, Humphrey Littleton is telling all: He will tell who the Jesuits were who talked him into becoming a plotter. Why, Father Hall (Oldcorne, he explains) is almost certainly hidden away in Hindlip, "at this present," and easily flushed out. Hall's, Oldcorne's, servant happens to be in Worcester jail, and he will know all. Show him the rack. The manacles. Littleton is getting carried away with vicarious cruelty. "After all," he adds, "Oldcorne said the plot was a good thing and long overdue. *Commendable* was his word." The Sheriff of Worcester at once stays his execution to see what else this tap of a man might yield up. After the top layer, there are many others, with truth at the bottom, tiny and glistening: a corm of fact.

In fact, Oldcorne had compared the plot to a pilgrimage made by Louis XI of France, in the course of which the plague erupted twice, wiping out most of his retainers the first time and killing Louis himself the next. His enemies came through unscathed. So much, Oldcorne said, for excursions organized by St. Bernard of Clairvaux. Someone flinched at the second syllable in Clairvaux, but no one spoke. "The principal thing," Father Oldcorne had said, "was what the expedition was for and how it was conducted. Many failures are honorable, and can only be judged by the moral good they bring about." Father Oldcorne still does not know what Catesby was trying to do. "It is between him and his God. Of course, I am against all reckless violence, sir." How easily, though, his words could be twisted into treason and treachery; between the inability to reveal what was said in confession and a general ignorance of the plot's aims, all priests were both unable to defend themselves and guilty to begin with.

To swell the general clamor, Mary Habington has her servants begin cleaning the household silver, tons of it, all dun and gray from disuse, and suddenly Sir Henry feels at home in the presence of a familiar ritual, as if in readiness for some social event, a banquet, say, and his mind saunters away from his reasons for being here and starts to dream of banquets, balls, near-orgies he himself has sponsored (they watch one another talk and listen to one another eat). The acrid tang of silver polish rises upstairs to the nostrils of Father Garnet, gagging and trying not to cough. He has been here since January 21. It is now Monday, January 27; it feels like years since Monteagle revealed the plot. He thinks he is going to faint as someone outside begins to hammer and grind. Surely this will be the ultimate discovery. He has no idea of what has happened to John Owen and Ralph Ashley, and he wonders if Anne has stayed on at Hindlip, convinces himself she has not. If not her, then, who has been sustaining them with warm broth sent through a long reed coming through the chimney? Was it not she who plied them with caudle, a food for invalids, succulent and sharp? Marmalade and candy they have provided for themselves, but that is all, and with the house in a state of perpetual siege from within there has been no chance of anyone's doing better. Their past week has been an elegy to egg and bacon, the aroma now overpowered by the reek of silver polish, the high acid content rising above everything else to tickle and scald the noses of those nearest.

"Well," says Garnet to Oldcorne, "shall we? I am choking, Edward."

"If we do, Henry, there will be no turning back. You well know how they proceed."

"Eternity in a byre," says Father Garnet. "Is this a perpetual penalty or have we earned our keep?"

"Our keep has always been free."

"*Ita vero.* Do we brave them, then?"

"Another day?"

"My gorge rises at the thought."

"Mine too. But shall we stay?"

"Shall we go out together?"

"To bathe and eat," Garnet echoes. Against their will, they take deep breaths and then have trouble uncoiling limbs. Then they impede each other, slithering out of that noxious narrow cupboard, Garnet coming out headfirst, his grievously swollen legs dragging behind him. He is an iguana, that ungainly. Oldcorne follows and, for a moment, they lie side by side, the old position, in the open, gasping and weeping tears of supreme effort mingled with self-disgust. "Were you ever in the one at Sawston," Garnet whispers. "I was," comes answer. "I know why you ask. There is an earth closet."

"Just so," says Henry Garnet, feeling like an incontinent school-boy who has messed his pants during Latin grammar and will soon be thrashed, given a good hiding (he winces) once he has been scrubbed. "With one of those close-stools," he murmurs, only inches from the stone floor, "we could have endured another three months. If we had only been able to get outside for an hour, we could have set ourselves up in there for life, with a folding altar and everything." He feels cheated: A brilliant idea has died at the hands of crass matter. "Oh to stand," he sighs.

"Or to stretch," Oldcorne adds, rising to kneel.

They both have a look of stunned arthritics, unshaven and wan and shattered. They are the palest priests in or near Worcester, not as pale as Guido Fawkes, but victims of stilled blood.

"Ho," says Sir Henry, "who *are* these stinking fellows?"

The team of poursuivants, briefly dipping face into the hole, recoil, heaving and gurgling, and then move away from the two priests, who stand unsteadily in barbaric isolation. Anne Vaux, horrified and weeping, keeps her distance, marveling that a mere week can reduce a human to such an abominable pass. Sir Henry, sensing the situation requires a summary comment, says, "They have been undone by those customs of nature which must of necessity be attended to. Those little vital commoners of the body keep us all in slavery to them, requiring that we absterge the podex, ladies and gentlemen. These wretched prelates have squatted in there with the devil himself and he has paid them back. Who do we have, then? Do you have names or do you just make noises? Are you well enough to answer? Shall we wash you?" Anne Vaux volunteers, but it is a motley crew of Hargreaves and some six searchers holding their noses who escort the two priests to an alcove on the ground floor, to which water can be brought, and clouts that can be thrown away as infested, infected loathsomes. The water-bringing servants squeal in horror and hasten to wash their own hands and faces. Anne Vaux knows now that the rationale of the hiding place has another side she has never thought of. It was folly to feed these men at all or to succor them with liquid. A weeklong sleep, she decides, next time, like that—what is it, the polar bear in somebody's play, when I was a civilized woman living a social life? *Sub cardine glacialis ursae*—usually she would ask Father Garnet and he would know, but not today. What does it mean? The rising of the ice? Ah, now I remember, 'tis the snowy Bear! Her mind has eased itself a little, unable to hear any more about customs of nature, which, to be honest about it, nauseate her at the best of times, not per se but because the facilities impress her as primitive and gross; wood-ash and earth shoveled on the mire of the day. Pico, she recalls, says we stand in it to clutch at heaven. Pico was right. Now they are cleaner, Sir Henry is urging them along, he wants them in Worcester, but he seems oddly benign in his treatment of them. Perhaps he likes priests.

Sir Henry Bromley can hardly believe his luck, but he begins to lose faith in it when he questions Father Garnet. Hall, alias Father Oldcorne, he has no trouble identifying: A man with only one alias has no hypocrites among his friends, but someone such as Garnet, alias at least half a dozen other men, has been brilliantly dispersed and camouflaged. Certainly this emaciated, worn, shuddering person is not Mister Perkins, nor is he any kind of whoremaster or manual laborer (Bromley examines his almost silky palms).

"Are you a priest, sir?"

"I cannot lie before God."

"Well?"

"I am a colleague of this gentleman."

"Have you been rash enough ever to submit to a name, a single name?"

Father Garnet identifies himself in a listless monotone; Anne, eavesdropping behind a door, has never heard him sound so depleted, so dreary. Now she begins to understand the impact of month after month of hiding in abysmal quarters unfit for animals. She would like to start over and install him from the first in a luxurious apartment like the one they envisioned him having in Rome: a room full of sundials sheathed in gold satin. How reckless of me, she thinks. Now they know who he is, and what: Quite a catch. They are bound to let him go as guiltless. Look what brought him to this. She does a dry sob, blaming herself for making of him a constant fugitive.

NINE BOXES

Siri Hustvedt

1.

The adult appeared parenthetical
Through the small double pane
And the frost's ragged flowering.
Behind it, in a pharmaceutical vial, are
A violet feather and three blue beads.
They secure the map of constellations:
A peephole to our cosmology
Where the Medici princess bathes in bubbles
That move nowhere but stay afloat forever
Like marble.

2.

She is always on point—
To pirouette without turning, to suggest the movement only
At the entrance of the Hotel
Where the driver covers her with the stiff furs of legend
And the stellar showers are caught in mid-flight,
Like fastened sequins
On a yellow newspaper that reads into the corners
Behind an inert mechanical bird,
In a cell,
Lit by Perseus.

3.

The veins of the heavens are traced with seventy-nine
        reflected lines
From point to point,
From bloodless Andromeda
Preserved in the map like a demonstrative embryo
That floats, but never grows,
Conceived from the needles and short threads of the sewing basket
To the blues of an undying Swan Lake
Sunk in a damaged mirror,
Under chipped plaster like the frailty of a grandmother's
        Doll house,
Kept for all these years.

4.

The doll stands in a forest
In a dress
The color of tea stains,
With red in her cheeks, and lashes
On eyes that don't close—
Speckled with white
In an enamel snow storm that doesn't move her hair
But takes place undercover, in our stories,
Lying on the night table under a ruffled lamp shade
In a windowless place.

5.

Twined and entwined,
One of a pair in the charm of identical children,
Split in the spell of minutiae.
The photographed faces behind blue glass
Multiplied, so the sisters were mirrors
Of genetic coupling
(Recorded in the symmetry of Caelum's four stars).
The two are discovered in an embrace without breath,
One small pair of white arms
Doubled in the other.

6.

It is going backwards, isn't it?
Finding the amniotic night sprinkled
With the objects of later years,
Out of chronology or any breeze that might disturb
A sleeping princess, unseen in the rose castle.
She is not restless in her sleep,
But sleeps in the chilled air of the museum
Like a disembodied symptom,
Written down and recorded for future illnesses
And other cures.

7.

Glued to the globe's peeled surface
Is a railway ticket.
Someone was traveling to Milan, a child,
Now missing in a pink hotel
Where confetti dots the vacuum.
We have closed ourselves in here,
With a floor and ceiling to things,
But we have names for all the remnants of these boxed dreams,
Unlike the fetus who sleeps and wakes in the unlit reticule
Of two hearts.

8.

We have gotten our things together
Before the trip,
A small hoard of connected points
To answer the nebula
That cannot be made out tonight
Or any other night.
We have chosen our clusters
And have loved them like the letters and spoons,
Thimbles and little pieces of twine
Forgotten in the beloved's desk.

9.

They whisper,
Like those who see the dead in the same room:
Outlining the universe in a coffin.
It is strange to think that infinity has six sides.
Heaven is the cage of the cosmos,
Reduced to the minute and the placid,
Our reticulum visible in January,
Ten tiny lights on an oak lid,
Shining like glass where the world sleeps
In a cat's-eye.

THE GRAND HOTELS
Robert Coover

THE GRAND HOTEL NIGHT VOYAGE

The Grand Hotel Night Voyage, described in its brochure as "a soaring tower of dreams and visions for transient romantics with repressed desires and eventless lives," is the archetypal grand hotel, first of its kind and said to be the progenitor of all others. Originally designed as a colorful hot air balloon (thus its name), it acquired its pagodalike tower—at the time still under construction—as a consequence of an unexpected descent, although the lobby, with its caged tropical birds, its musical fountain, and its bright yellow walls, lined with mirrors, movie posters, and paintings of dancers and acrobats, retains still some of the lost balloon's original charm and gaiety. Indeed, this chance encounter of balloon and tower, so like that of hotel guests in, say, the elevator or common restrooms or the hair salon, not only brought the Grand Hotel Night Voyage into existence, but made fortuitous juxtaposition a standard requirement for grand hotel classification thereafter.

Though the lobby is ever aglitter with its myriad reflections, bright paint, and exotic plumage, however, there appears at check-in time, drifting in from stairwells, elevator shafts, and inner passages, a somber blue haze, faintly redolent of fresh cut paper and silver nitrate, and of grass made fragrant by evening dew: a reminder to visitors that the hotel, as its name suggests, is not for lighthearted day-trippers or busloads of convivial tourists, but for dedicated and solitary explorers of the night. There are no double beds in the Grand Hotel Night Voyage. Many of the rooms have no walls, it's true; or, better said, none of the rooms have walls all the time; but they do not communicate with one another. One may well meet fellow travelers in the night's migrations (one speaks of this not as a passing by but a passing through), but they will not necessarily be residents of the same hotel. For those who are regulars here, as are most, it is upon entering (or being entered by) this curling blue mist, not unlike the gas that once lifted the hot air balloon skyward, that one begins to feel at home.

Which is to say: back in the real world once more, safely removed from the impossible fantasy of one's own incomprehensible passage through what are known beyond the hotel as time and world. Behind the front desk, the bright open expanse of the lobby gives way to the comforting shadows of the intricately compartmentalized interior, with its ancient twisted staircases that rise and fall like heaving waves, its muffled whir and whisper of dreams past seeking to reconstitute themselves, and its meandering labyrinth of dark wainscoted corridors with their seemingly infinite series of dissolving and reemerging doors. Discreet night porters are available as guides and translators for the inexperienced, and room service offers a full range of scientific and whimsical instruments, mechanical devices, and recording equipment to assist all voyagers in their explorations. Which for many begin even before a room is entered, such peace and harmony do they find here. The pleasure felt by the travelers as they penetrate the hotel's innermost recesses is reciprocal: The hotel, too, seems to experience a profound elemental harmony as it fills with guests, and, as the night deepens, the entire Grand Hotel Night Voyage, afloat now in its rich blue fog, begins slowly to expand and contract as if taking great reposeful breaths.

THE GRAND HOTEL PENNY ARCADE

At the very heart of the Grand Hotel Penny Arcade, encased in blue glass and pale as porcelain, floats a sleeping princess, gracefully coiling and uncoiling, clothed only in her own purity, her eyes open but unseeing. Her slow liquid movements, contained in an architecture that is both formal and evocative, are those of a sleepwalker: elaborate, balletic, silent, unrelated to her austere geometric surroundings. Though she is, as seen, a lonely figure, she does not seem to suffer from loneliness. She appears much of the time to find herself amid imagined multitudes, waving, greeting friends, dancing, eating, posing, petting a dog or cat, climbing into a car, disembarking a train, shopping, lifting children onto horses or carnival rides, or being lifted. Yet, there is an element of shy restraint in even her most open gestures, the suggestion of an innocent child's uncertainty in the face of the rude world, and an unwillingness to embrace it fully, as if to do so might awaken her from the private world in which she so restfully and winsomely resides. She is both utterly exposed yet secretive, transparent yet evasive and mysterious. The princess of solitude.

The guest rooms of the hotel, all decorated in marine blue and permeated with the faint sweet aroma of youthful flesh, encircle the sleeping princess on several levels, each room with its own individual coin-operated peephole viewers, viewers technically augmented by manual zoom lenses, tracking and lock-on mechanisms worked with a crank, and simulated kinetoscopic flickering. As the princess is never completely still, or almost never, no room is particularly privileged, so room rates are the same for all, though each visitor is known to have her or his preference. Although some first-timers feel compelled by nature to zoom in on her private parts, so-called (the princess's private parts, as they eventually discover, are all hidden deeply within), most

viewers come to prefer close-ups of her face, thrilled by the illusion
that the dreamer is sometimes gazing directly at them as if in recognition, or else they select more distant views of her whole figure, in
movement or at rest. The classic perspective. Some leave their rooms
to take in the full panorama from the open galleries on the top level,
while others prefer not to watch at all, but only to be told what others
are seeing that they might more fully imagine her. "What is she doing
now?" "It's as if she were playing in a schoolyard, skipping rope!"
"Describe the movements of her arms and legs!" "Do you not want to
hear about her little breasts?" "First, her arms and legs!" Day or night,
the deep blue of the hotel's interior and the subdued lighting create a
reflective nocturnal mood, making stays at the Grand Hotel Penny
Arcade seem more like séances, as some have said when signing the
guestbook: "It felt like an encounter with my own lost soul. I shall
return again and again." Slowed-down, melancholic movie house
organ tunes can be heard during viewings, but, though associated with
the princess's languid movements, they emerge more as sourceless
room aura, a device incorporated by the architect to make the
admirers of the princess feel a part of what they are witnessing, rather
than mere voyeurs.

The accusation of voyeurism, it must be said, has hovered over
the hotel since its opening. Hailed in the travel and arts journals as an
architectural triumph and a must-stop for all travelers ("The Grand
Hotel Penny Arcade restores risk and ingenuity to architecture,
managing an air of sophistication without ostentation, charm without
quaintness, truth without didacticism, as it strives heroically toward an
abstract ideal of feminine beauty and structural harmony…"), it was
at the same time in the tabloids the subject of scurrilous cartoons and
prurient rumors. In those days, many men and some women ventured
here, hoping to awaken the dancing sleeper with whatever it took, and
others came to watch this happen, but all left chastened by the aware-
ness that not only was she a princess who did not await a prince, she
was, even in her doll-like nakedness, the very image of eternal innocence, eliciting not carnal desire but profound awe and affection and

something, mysteriously, like hope. Indeed, were she clothed, as the architect noted in his famous homily on the transcendent radiance of her buttocks, and of the buttocks of women in general, she would immediately be dated and placed, and he wanted her to remain forever universal and timeless.

Even with the fading of the controversy, however, some questions have remained. Is she, for example, as claimed in the hotel brochure, alive, or is she some kind of elaborate automaton, a projection, in effect, of the architect's fantasy? And if alive, how did she come upon her strange fate and will she ever be released from it, even if she does not want to be? On the other hand, if she, who seems more alive than any of those watching her, is not alive, then what are they? Anxiety-arousing questions, bordering, in short, on the realm of the uncanny. Which may speak to the architect's genius for provocation; or it may speak to his confusion. For his adoration of his structural centerpiece has seemed to go beyond mere aesthetics. He is known, when she is the subject, to speak, not only of form and function, body and move-ment, but of tenderness, generosity, pathos, sincerity, and an ineffable longing for a lost past, almost as if she had ceased being a structural component of his architectural inventions and had become the object, in a word, of his amorous obsession. Has what began as artistic adven-ture and celebration become, for him as well as for her, inescapable entrapment? If so, then what is for guests an enriching and consoling connection to the eternal verities (as advertised in the hotel brochure), is for the architect, who is not known to have constructed anything since the Grand Hotel Penny Arcade, a tragic estrangement.

THE GRAND HOTEL GALACTIC CENTER

The most courageous of the grand hotels is the Grand Hotel Galactic Center, home of the Big Bang Milk Bar, the Transcendental Massage Parlor, and the Celestial Ballet, performed nightly, hotel weather per-mitting. It is approached by way of a labyrinth of narrow twisted streets, a maze that often thwarts the novice, making the hotel, which is in the very heart of the city, seem mythic and remote, improbable even. Once found, however, it has a startling *thereness* that can never ever after be entirely avoided, its compelling curves catching the eye at almost any turning. For the architect has here abandoned the traditional stacking of windowed blocks, with their sober geometry of grid-like patterning and their compartmentalized rooms and corridors like button boxes or museum cases, in favor of a structure built entirely of translucent interlocking spheres, creating the illusion of a great cosmic vastness within an architectural space said to be the smallest of all the grand hotels. A feature of the hotel, much ballyhooed in its brochure ("Practical Hints"), is that every room has an overhead view of the night sky, though there is some suspicion, never proved, that this is occasionally accomplished with mirrors and projectors. The sky is exposed each evening at sundown with the slow drawing back of what the hotel calls its "cloud cover," much as sheets might be pulled away from a freshly made bed, bringing on a spectacle described by guests as "awesome," "heart-stopping," "elemental," and "big!"

This theme of cosmic grandeur is carried out throughout the hotel, from the twinkling fairy lights suspended everywhere in background black light and the T. M. Parlor with its gravity-free rubdown bubble-rooms ("Out of the body through the body!") to the hotel elevators, which seemingly lift their passengers on small platforms through the opening immensity of the Milky Way. At the top is the Big Bang Milk Bar, in reality an automat diner offering packaged food and soda pop, for the regulars at the Grand Hotel Galactic Center care little for passing gustatory pleasures, their minds being wholly on the permanent, the infinite. Sensualists find even the transcendental massages disappointing, as no hands are used, only subtle changes in atmospheric pressure within the spinning white bubbles wherein the massaged serenely float. A deep silence reigns throughout the hotel, broken only by a faint electric crackle and the hushed murmurs, as the cloud cover is pulled back, of awed guests.

Of course, gazing fixedly upon infinity is not without its risks. If the guestbook is to be believed, many have been driven mad by it, though it's equally possible they were already somewhat crazed, or at least eccentric, when, drawn by the alluring sadness, the alluring terror, they first came here. Others have simply disappeared as though swallowed up by the hotel itself, causing some to believe that the old joke about the black hole at the core of the bubbly edifice might not be a joke after all. The staff smilingly deny it, though even they will admit that the hotel's peculiar arrangement of intersectored spheres, some visible, some invisible, has necessarily left occasional spiky voids, tiny irregular patches of negativity, which they insist, however, are harmless. Unfortunately, these rumored disappearances and structural anomalies have lured to the Galactic Center persons intent not on contemplation but on suicide, and these sad gray figures can be seen at all hours, even during performances of the Celestial Ballet, drifting melancholically through the silent hotel, feeling the walls for unmarked passages and secret doors, falling asleep in the massage bubbles, lingering near air shafts and leaning against the starry walls of the elevators, hoping to get sucked painlessly into the arms of dark eternity.

Though not completely successful, and having acquired over the years a weathered, timeworn look unsuited to the purity of its quest (partly due to reckless abuse from some of the guests, especially the anarchic young, in whom the grandeur of the cosmos all too often inspires wild and irresponsible behavior), the hotel nevertheless still expresses much of the architect's original noble desire to provide the guests—through an exuberant display of classical form conjoined with clarity of vision and an eye for the absolute—a certain architectonic reassurance, stimulation, serenity, inspiration. "Reverie and revelation," as the brochure says. It was perhaps this emphasis on the spiritual that led to the hotel's well-known material defects, serious enough for it to be in constant danger of losing one or more of its stars and being downgraded to the Petit or Ordinary Hotel Galactic Center.

The furnace room is said to be particularly dangerous, for example, and the building, under perpetual reconstruction due to the lack of a sustaining kingpost and weak foundations, has virtually nonexistent emergency exit facilities and suffers frequent power failures. But in spite of its—admittedly fundamental—flaws, the Galactic Center retains, thanks to the architect's whimsical genius of expression, a prevailing and compensatory lightheartedness, such that a night spent in it can be both majestic and frivolous, terrifying and consoling, deranging and healing, harmonious and chaotic. As one guest (who, alas, later disappeared) put it: "The Galactic Center: C'est moi."

THE GRAND HOTEL FORGOTTEN GAME

Unlike many of the other grand hotels, the Grand Hotel Forgotten Game is as easy to find as closing one's eyes and opening them again. The front desk, on the other hand, is deeply concealed within a labyrinth of movable panels of wood and glass and is shifted about from hour to hour, making checking into the hotel the first game one is obliged to play here, though by no means the most difficult. It is child's play compared, for example, to finding one's room afterwards. At the entrance, on the revolving doors (which are tricky; not every-one gets inside on the first try), there is posted a quotation, attributed to a 19th-century saint, that reads: "Now, *here*, you see, it takes all the running *you* can do, to keep in the same place." Though newcomers might be baffled by such an announcement, Forgotten Game regulars understand it to be a clue, by reverse logic, to finding the front desk: Locate yourself in a safe place and let the front desk come to you.

The rooms, however, can be accessed only by Ferris wheels and carousels (there are no elevators, stairs, or ordinary corridors, though one learns to recognize certain playgrounds and amusement parlors as secret routes of passage), such that the odds of being dropped off at one's room are about the same as those of winning at roulette. Nor is reaching one's door—if one ever does—the end of the game, for inserting the key can cause the floor in front of the door to drop away (the guessing and singing of "the song of the day" while inserting the key can prevent this) and send the guest flying down a ramp of wooden rollers past holes in the wall at which other guests are shooting with paint guns. The chute continues all the way to the bottom of the hotel, where it releases the splattered guest into the alleyway at the back, and the process begins all over again.

The hotel staff are all delightfully charming and kind, given to generous laughter, warm embraces, and amusing aphorisms, and playing hide-and-seek with the chambermaids and bellhops is not only encouraged, it is the only way to get breakfast or have your bed made, but it is useless to ask them for directions or advice when lost in the hotel. Not only are they instructed to provide only false clues and misinformation, many of them are deceivingly lifelike automata, programmed to provide random replies no matter what the questions. But clues are to be found everywhere; one need only look and sensibly puzzle out what one sees. Even the patterns of the colored sand in the sandboxes may provide directions, or the worn areas of carpets, the casual spray of jacks or marbles, the squawk of a parrot, candy wrappers behind a chair, a stack of alphabet blocks. At some point, one will probably lose track of one's luggage, but once the room is found there will be luggage in it, probably not one's own, but no matter. People dressing up in one another's clothes is part of the hotel policy to get everyone playing together. Mail and messages are not delivered but are hidden about the hotel like Easter eggs, finders keepers, and indeed Easter bunnies (live and otherwise) are a cheerful decorative motif throughout. The restaurant menus are playing cards, and one must find a guest with a matching card before one can be served—as a pair, of course. The menus themselves list no dishes, only conundrums, such as What is the color of surprise? or Where exactly is the universe? or If time runs, where does it run to? or What does an egg mean? and the guests are served according to their answers, usually to their complete satisfaction. There are costume parties every night, if one can find them, with dancing contests and sack races and sing-alongs. The playful atmosphere has provoked new games, invented by the guests, like goosey gander, nipple tag, and musical beds, but these innovations are not encouraged by the management, and such guests often find themselves suddenly shooting the chutes once more and landing in the alley.

The colors in the Grand Hotel Forgotten Game are mostly primary, the ambient music that of a rollicking hurdy-gurdy, and the dispersed aromas range from those of ice cream parlors and fireworks to hot asphalt, pencil sharpeners, and the seaside, depending on where one finds oneself in the hotel, and when. Indeed, there is, though not easy to find, a seaside beach somewhere in the hotel where the hurdy-gurdy melodies fade away behind the sounds of sand and pebbles sucking sea water, waves slapping against wooden piers, and the cries of wheeling gulls. There are shellfish expeditions here, daily beach parties featuring sand castle building and blindman's buff on the boardwalk, and fishing competitions from the piers, where one catches not fish but fortunes, and sometimes toy cars or plastic earrings. Transoceanic excursions can be arranged for guests on extended stays, with overnights in the Tropical Island Beach Hut, which can also be reached by taking the Ferris wheel to the sixth floor, if one can find it (it is not between the fifth and seventh).

At the top of the hotel in the middle of a set of Chinese boxes is the Game Room (this is not the casino, which is called The Schoolyard), where management and staff meet with the design team to plot out each day's activities and the structural adjustments required. It is here that all the jokes and riddles are dreamed up and the fun invented. It is widely assumed (the hotel's publicity department encourages this public assumption) that these Game Room meetings are the happiest games of all at the Grand Hotel Forgotten Game, yet witnesses who have stumbled onto the Game Room looking in vain for their own rooms have reported dim lights, a heavy air faintly redolent of old shoes and books, and a prevailing mood of inwardness and preoccupation, melancholy, wistfulness, in which, say, the blowing of a soap bubble would be a cause for tears.

THE GRAND HOTEL NYMPHLIGHT

Although childhood is the source and model of all architecture, grand hotels included, the Grand Hotel Nymphlight is the only one known to be specifically devoted to "the child within," as the hotel brochure puts it. Uniquely situated—it is in reality a hotel within a hotel—the Grand Hotel Nymphlight features all-glass construction, playhouse dimensions, dreamlike décor, common dormitories and restrooms, and, through innovative engineering, the literal re-experience of one's own lost childhood. The universal desire to be a child again, full of innocent wonder and spontaneity and extravagant joy (as advertised), while yet knowing what one knows as an adult, is realized at check-in time, when, by way of a warm bath administered by the hotel staff, the guests are returned for twenty-four hours to their prepubescent physical and spiritual condition, free of all adult anxieties and repressions and perversities, albeit wiser in the ways of the world, dressed in their own clothing from that time, if they have supplied it, else from clothing specially fashioned for them from photographs, and sent out to play with other children their seeming age or, if they wish, to enter into and explore their own pasts in an interactive museum whose exhibits change with each new set of guests.

Admission into the Grand Hotel Nymphlight is not easily obtained, not only because it is the most popular of all the grand hotels, booked up months, even years, in advance, but also because those seeking entry are required to provide a vast array of support materials to assist the engineering staff in all their recreative tasks, including photographs and films, drawings, clothing, games and toys, dolls, balls, uniforms, comic books, names and types of pets, and lists of everything from childhood sports and hobbies, favorite foods, books, and movies to happiest and saddest moments, secret childtime wishes, dreams. Merely to have kept or remembered all these things is enough to suggest that the prospective guest who supplies them is ideally suited for an overnight in the hotel. There are many, of course, who long for such an experience but who have few or no support materials to offer, and, though it is against hotel policy, they often borrow these things from others or buy new. They thereby relive a childhood they never knew—one probably more delightful than their own forgotten one, for delight is the principal aim of the hotel—whereupon their night in the Grand Hotel Nymphlight becomes in effect their "true memory" of childhood. As it ought, for to be without any other is a sad thing. All guests must leave behind some of the support materials they have brought—usually a toy plus an article or two of clothing—as partial payment for their stay, and these items become the property of the hotel management. Children who are children now are also admitted, and much more freely, partly to intensify the experience of the children from other times, but also simply because they are loved. For them, the room rates are exceptionally low, especially if unaccompanied by an adult, usually little more than a frock, a shirt, a hairband or bracelet, a toy. Thus, one cannot be sure if it is a real child one is playing with or an adult reliving her childhood, and this is part of the joy and wonder of it all.

If the playhouse dimensions make full-grown adults feel ill at ease, that was probably the original intention of the architect, though it was also necessary to create a structure that would fit comfortably and unobtrusively within the Hotel Lost Domain, which embraces it; not itself one of the grand hotels, being imitative (neo-Gothic in a depressed sort of way) and of little architectural significance, yet nearly as popular as the hotel which it contains, and especially with the elderly. The Hotel Lost Domain has but one compellingly attractive feature, which is the sole reason for its popularity: All its rooms peer in upon the Grand Hotel Nymphlight. From them, one can immerse oneself all day in the magical world of children—and all night, too, for what is more pleasurable than watching, unwatched, sleeping boys and girls, their dreams on view like ghostly videos? Some of the Lost Domain clientele are virtually permanent residents, but others include prospective and past guests of the Nymphlight, as well as friends and loved ones of the current guests. Couples usually check in to the Nymphlight to play together on this one chance in life that they have, especially lovers of different ages who for a night can be, together, ten again, but some go singly, their partners taking a room in the Lost Domain to revel in the sight of their beloved in the shape of a playing child.

Is there, as is sometimes rumored, another hotel embracing the Lost Domain, wherein watchers watch the watchers and the watched as well? No, that's more likely just a fantasy of the popular press, one metaphor propagating another in the common way, though as a safety precaution the security staff of the Nymphlight does have cameras in place in both hotels. Not that there is much risk of dangerous or unseemly behavior. There is probably no hotel in the world more chaste in its design and policy with respect to children than the Grand Hotel Nymphlight, none more devoted to innocence, purity, and simple childish delight. Even the nightmares are largely avoided, their screenings interrupted with sweet motherly murmurs, and though murder, rape, war, cruelty, torture, beatings, abuses, and horrors of every sort are common experiences of preadolescence everywhere, there's little of any of that here, unless specifically introduced in the memorabilia of a guest, for these things are of the world without, not the child within. The residents of the Lost Domain, however, are not so scrupulously screened as those in the Nymphlight, and the sight of a hotelful of ruddy little smooth-skinned cherubs, candidly doing all the little things they do, can be improperly arousing to perverse or weak natures. Even among divided lovers, there can arise an irresistible urge to break through the glass barrier to embrace one's lover, deliciously virginal again. The children, however, are always completely safe from outsiders, protected by the glass firewall that divides the grown-up hotel from the inner child's hotel, such that even though there have been rare occasions of obscene public behavior, they have been mostly out of view of the young and seeming young.

No, the true dangers of the Grand Hotel Nymphlight lie more in the intrusion upon one's own childhood without the grace of childhood ignorance, for it is not always a good thing (how often we tell children this!) to obtain what one most desires. One may have prepared oneself before checking in for the possible unearthing of forgotten fears and anxieties, not least those of the playground, and one might even have foreseen that some of the most joyous moments in the hotel would, at the same time, knowing what one knows, be profoundly melancholic, augmenting rather than relieving one's sense of loss (some little guests, playing their hearts out, weep the while, as children often do), but one cannot anticipate the panic that can seize a guest who suddenly, too late, repents of his or her decision. Sometimes this happens already in the bath, but, even though this may give rise to a great thrashing about, there is no undoing what has begun until its full course has been run. Others, momentarily entranced by the seductive pleasures of the bath, are struck by terror only upon entering into the company of the other children, and terrified not by the others but by their own strange, confused, and diminished selves, by their appalling and ruthless innocence, discovering in that instant that, while losing one's childhood can be a sad thing, losing one's adulthood, even for a day (if it's only a day! what is happening? I can't remember!), can be catastrophic. Twenty-four hours is a long time, and to the restored child gripped by irrational panic it can seem forever. Of course, such exceptions cannot be allowed to spoil the fun for others. The hotel's procedures for managing these episodes are mostly pharmaceutical and mostly successful, though somewhat at the expense of the guest's pleasure, or his or her memory of it.

FOR BROTHER ROBERT

Bradford Morrow

And then I heard them lift a box,
And creak across my soul
With those same boots of lead, again.
Then space began to toll ...
—EMILY DICKINSON

THE WINTER DAY was as plain as flour paste, and outside your window the sunlight was of the same whiteness as your walls and ceiling. The moon had abandoned the sky the night before, and stars hid behind the haze. No meteors had fallen for us to esteem. Simply, the dead calm of your brother's birthday reigned over this morning, as it had before dawn when night is at its most impervious depth. And all this plain white emptied scape provoked a spirited proposition, an inducement to one whose sole thoughts until then turned to you, and were sorry leaden things, sunken cakes, silent and without shape.

Mild morning December light made the grass look chalky, like dried milk, out in our backyard. Our quince tree, too, was white and reminded us of a carving in ivory. The blanched chairs we arranged back there at certain angles cast flat white shadows on the white lawn. The slow air—which toured our leaky house and traveled the yard and walked up into the quince tree, where it was cooled by the ghosts of songbirds and by the dazzling wintry sun—appeared to be white-washed and rubbed. Robert, we were young. Mother was strong, our sisters were young. You were especially strong in your frailty. The world, too, was tenuous and promising only insofar as it was an empty white box. Thin air coveted this box and, through its silences, declared both itself and the box that held it unfulfilled. The birds might have echoed this dilemma with warning cries in the ivory quince, had they not abandoned us to such stifling quiet. I strained without success to hear their tolling.

No time passed. Not a day, nor a fortnight, nor a year. All but the balmy, gone birds remained the same, as we thought, What to do? What to do?

You remember, dear Robert, old owl, that when they migrated months ahead of schedule that particular year, they left behind a pasteboard parrot in their wake—a collective gesture meant as a kindness, surely, but who could ever be sure? Meant perhaps to soothe those whom they'd fled—who could blame them? I did not—and left us alone in our clapboard house, left our garden chair beneath that tree, slumbering in old, abundant solitude. What did those many birds mean by such gestures of leaving? You said, although you might not have said it in just these words: Birds only partly succeed in fulfilling certain half-finished thoughts and half-made promises, since, now, aren't we reminded once more of how silent and colorless the world can be without them in it? Whereas the breathing world may feel their absence, we feel the difficult presence of their not being in the quince, or under the eaves or on this windowsill.

So you said, Robert, on that plainest day, that once. And though there were no cardinals or jays in the boughs for my Christmas Eve birthday we decided the tree should not be cut down.

Paste real wings on the treacherous parrot but it would not fly away. Or so you tell me and so I believe you. Look at it, proud there, pretty and arrogant and anything but dumbfounded, with its evidently orange beak, and with feathers so blue they bring tears to your eyes and to the eyes of Mother and Helen and Elizabeth, too. You say, Let's keep it. I don't see these blues and oranges but keep my blindness to myself. The parrot seemed to be low maintenance, as pets go, and so I agreed, nodding. You noted my silence in the matter even as you swore the parrot was not colorless, let alone invisible. It perched on your ceiling that morning, observing us just as you watched it, our mother and sisters staring upward, too. Live and let live, I thought, but wondered if we were to be its keepers or its pets, wondered if we weren't the invisibles, while parrot, Chinese quince, the sunless sky beyond your constant bed, and even the narrow yard below were the truer presences.

Visible or not, this parrot did display no interest in the crackers I set out on the newspaper, near the cage that I had made for it out of wooden clothes hangers—remember? Remember how I wanted to paint the parrot's beak a dark orange to suggest my deeper yearning, but could not? Even the water in the clear little plastic bowl hung inside the cage evaporated before the parrot had any chance to consider whether thirst might motivate it to drink. Shall I paint the water blue?

You heard my questions but only smiled, so I sat out in the backyard in my overcoat and waited for another color to come to mind. None came just then. Mother helped you down so you could sit beside me, Robert. It was then you suggested that today, my birthday, proposed an idea, one that might develop into other ideas. Today, yes today, you continued. Today we won't be staying home like we always do because today is your birthday, and so we will go traveling, like air, like songbirds.

I reminded you I wasn't fond of birthdays—they represented death's knell—reminded you that you were hesitant of leaving the house. You insisted, however. You wanted me to see something. And now I must confess, Robert. You were courageous, our mother was strong and our sisters were young, our poor father, though gone to heaven, was capable, and the world was shallow, hollow, insubstantial but promising insofar as it was yet an empty white box. How reluctant I was to break the trance cast by that quince, the mansard-roofed bayside house, the fenced yard.

Yes, I said. Go we will, and the parrot can eat or drink and if not, die. So we studied your maps, we talked and planned and as we did, the journey came toward us even as we inclined toward it. This was not to be some usual trip. But we admitted to a shared passion about the proposed excursion, which seemed to involve magnificent trains. And weren't we delighted when the parrot descended from the ceiling and became a part of our more common world? It seemed a sign that all boded well and through the quick of my tedious doubts it cut.

Pasted with fondness, or do they say plastered, we were going to attend a holiday parade. It was early afternoon and you were mad with merriment and clapping your gloved hands for effect, knowing that while I have never cherished vivid displays of celebration, I would not break my promise to go.

Nothing would rain, sleet or snow on our parade today, I thought, still the nonpareil worst birthday celebrant ever. I dressed myself and helped you dress. We put on birthday hats and set out together to range across the field of dead flowers, leaves and bramble, going forth to the station in town under an abundant sky of pure anonymity. No snow today, I thought again, but rather some interior mist, like a private grief hidden behind my hundred honest frowns. Mist like that which we remember rising sometimes from the Hudson back when we lived in Nyack. This, and the certainty of the very slow progress of typical marching bands, the same old floats, some several clowns, some majorettes, and a variety of other wondrous, monstrous stuff at the end of the happy line.

Mother of course accompanied us, Elizabeth and Helen too, and foursquare we brought along thoughts of home and the quince tree in the yard and the chairs under the tree by the fence out back. Not to mention the hibernating rosebush there, which we might have strung with lights had we not gone on this excursion.

Our train ride was uneventful. We listened to the clacking of the steel wheels on the tracks. I bought hot coffee in the cafe car, and brought you tea with an old slice of lemon, no sugar. We passed a pleasant time together, then discovered we were there, having arrived along the main street of just another modest town—representatives, all of us, of the slow progress of being living souvenirs on a plain day, a day as common as a gift of a box full of worthless cutout artifacts given by a boy to his brother, his mother, his sisters, his friends—or else given to nobody. Here was Main Street in an ordinary town on an ordinary day, naked in its ordinariness. This is what you said and I believed you.

You said my gift to you—like yours to me—of coming outside into the world was a good gift, but that sometimes the giver can be confounded by what may come from out of the blue (euphemism yours) in return.

I thought about that, but said nothing again, having nothing to give you back. So we traded bodies, and traded them again, as we rolled through town hoping to find a good place where we might sit on the curb and watch the parade. We rolled with sisters and mother (and maybe father's ghost) on through this modest town that put me in mind of boxes populated by emptiness. Rows of complex boxes reflecting the colorless clouds that limped along overhead, no prouder than the dry rags they were. Dry white rags of clouds that were young back then, but nevertheless dry as that parrot's beak back home, from cardboard carefully cut.

Past, olden music strikes up, now, a tin horn somewhere, and a drum snares. A yuletide melody maybe. A horse carries the parade master,

who has lost one of his polished liturgical boots in some other prome-
nade. A leaden grin plays at his lips—theirs, in fact, both horse's and
master's. A large candelabra on the starlet's head and another on the
dunce's, all their many wicks burning bright. What a show, I begin to
think, as we settle in to watch with the rest, people standing and people seated around us. The large, meditative crowd laughs and claps as
the horse, master, starlet and dunce plod forward somehow, the
horse's white coat having now turned chestnut brown, whereupon you
ask me did I see what happened? Did I see the starlet blush as the
dunce winked?

You know I have no answer and so don't question my silence. We
know one another pretty well, being brothers. Nor do Mother or
Helen or Liz or the ghost of our father intervene, being as they are
quite caught up in the grandeur and hilarity of the procession.

Now a fish is next, exotic, raising its fist not in defiance but as to
hold aloft a striped orange and black balloon. And in the yellow wicker basket of this great balloon, a crew of foreign dignitaries is sipping
champagne, it would appear. Top hats and tails on the gentlemen, who
have fiery eyes; and a filigreed gown on the lady, whose face is a sin-
cerely beautiful steam locomotive. Like parrots and bits of ancient
lace—like the house and quince and lawn chair and rosebush back
home, and like you yourself, old owl Robert—trains are truly beautiful. And this one is glossy black with silver trim. Imagine that.

Hooplas and huzzahs from the crowd for what comes along next.
I miss whatever it was, but it doesn't matter, because I glance at you,
bearing witness to your growing contentment, and this is gift enough
for me. I witness contentment in our mother's face, too, and in
others'—enough, or almost enough.

Cut, paste, carve, you say. Arrange, rebalance. Go on, you say. Put
your hands to the scene itself.

Proud as punch next come senators, fresh mollusks, highway
patrolmen, gymnastic almanacs, waving cabriolets, pimps juggling
clementines, caribou and zombies, the major himself and other deities,

together in a feathered swan float, singing some mahogany chorale. Thereafter, devils and angels and curious harlot pumpkins. The alphabet block, the toy Judy, the commemorative spoon from Marseilles. The wicker fence percussion band, look and listen. The Golconda beyond my power to deem. Robin Hood in a nightgown is here, and so are the many marbles in his head. A Wassily chair waltzes the Matilda. Music by Glück, Mussorgsky and an acanthus leaf in frosty flames beyond the reach of any mathematician. Pennies are forged by various dirty vendors along the route, beside the burgeoning road, and other pennies are lost. The marionettes carry shards of glass gingerly and gingerly again. Whistles blow pink smoke as a huge Catherine's wheel twirls away above and beyond the history of all technology. But, more. Whales' teeth follow between the sleep and the sleep, eating the wild dust of other gadgets while they go. Nothing is a third wheel. Everything tells a story and the story is that everything tells the story.

A wooden crate is carried along, now that we near the end of the procession, held by hands too burdened by the weight of it to count. A candid hush falls over the crowd. It comes, it goes, and we are left behind in thrall as the choir within it of mockingbirds, borzois, gazelles and the rest of a comprehensive bestiary launched into some haunting song of faith that promises like decoupage a kind of richness, in which reveling in detail becomes a feast of experience.

Robert, how we both cut up.

Pastel weather begins to depreciate further chances for continued exposition, and these hundred fat bears on tricycles bring up the rear. One musician Cupid seems to have lost a wing and lies on his side, ignored by everyone but us—we who go to him where he's fallen in the broomed dirt lane—and while it is true that he courageously waves us off, preferring his agony to our charity, his remaining wing does seem to twitch. Not so bad, you say.

Won't he be forced to fly in circles from now on, though, given that he has but one wing? I ask.

We all fly in circles, you answer. It goes on, you say, it goes on just fine, and I believe you because we're brothers. Better one healthy wing than none, you add.

This makes me smile, and I begin to think, Robert, as the sun dims down and the last train to Utopia Parkway awaits us at the station, whatever it was we saw this day, you seem to be more fortunate for it, or fortuned by it. Mother and sisters more fortunate, our dead father, and I more fortunate, as we say goodbye to the modest town of boxes less empty than I might have imagined, and watch the landscapes slide by us beyond the scratched windows of the train taking us home, retracing our way toward that unplush shoebox where the rosebush, the arranged chairs, the birdhouse on the fence, the quince, and all the growing collection in my head of precious artifacts made by hands of mortals, and, yes, the very idea of home, await us.

Not to mention our monastic parrot, or is it a parakeet?

Passing under Utopia's horizon, the sun had gone. You asked me did I remember that turquoise elephant which, during the parade, danced on a glass bubble blown by a mauve butterfly? Whereas I could not remember such an elephant, nor bubble, nor butterfly, I knew if I opened my eyes I could imagine such things.

You misquoted our mutual favorite poet that evening after we finished dinner. Some days, you said,

> *Some days as if they were*
> *People or trains or sleepy quince*
> *Trees, do retire to rest, and*
> *In soft distinction lie*
> *Or tell some various truth.*

That day had been good for a birthday, truth to tell, after all. That day changed the shape and color of our house, and any world beyond.

Robert, how young we were. Mother, sisters, even Father. The world was young, going to war yet on its way back from war. Promising as an emptied, empty, emptying box. Whistling as the formerly unsung air toured it, the world and the box that was the world, soughing like someone breathing, and how it declared this little universe could be fulfilled, and you agreed with the speaking chill breeze that promised the empty box would be filled with fresh minutiae from your life, from mine, from every life ever lived.

I came along to see the parade at your kind invitation and this is my letter of gratitude. If I hadn't been there, it would have mattered. But I was there, for you, and you, old friend, old owl, were there for me. A parade of amazements. Life enclosed in an intoxicating turbine casket.

More, you say. There's more.

Yes, the moon is somewhat edged by a pale orchid, though my eyes are exhausted and my mind may be playing tricks to trump me. Too, there might be truth in what you saw in dusklight—several warblers, crisply carved and brazenly painted, returning to their nests, having tired of the heat of untimely climates. It may be true their breasts are speckled black on yellow, and that some of them are dappled with reds and greens and blues. But by what magic did those cracker crumbs vanish while we were away?

Birds. What more is there to confess? The December day was plain as paste no longer and I knew what color to cut in for the parrot's beak and so did you. The beak was, like the day, the fortnight, the year, the world, unhinged, forever quince and blue and green and gray and red and black and orange and white and every known color and unknown and simply: *bird.*

The parrot is animate, beautiful, always bright. As are the quince, the moon, the yard, and the house in which we dwelled together all those unforgotten years. Or so we tell ourselves and thus we believe, being brothers, being believers as we are and will be, opening and never closing our crypts of cutouts, and the pasts, nows and futures they manifest. That night, before you slept, we saw meteors lighting the sky, flying like wings outside your flaring window. From the starry dark an impossible nightingale sang you to your rest.

MAGIC MUSÉE
Martine Bellen

1.

She, who's over-conscious of her cage
Formed from heat, moisture, frost, concealment,

How it drips, freezes, fogs
How it forms columnar cracks gashed with glass

Toward the blue peninsula, gravity flight
The visible half of reflection

Attempting to obtain the solidity of an object

Or to remove the clothing of sound, genealogical anxiety,
Disrobing at the Hotel Eden

Inventing a way in
To that which is built over concept

2.

Behold, Thoreau sings for owls, Dickinson hummingbirds
Still life enframes world of spectacle

Or object-spirits

Dewish   mute

The Pyramids are letters, some die inside
Cul-de-sac feelings or Stonehenge numbers
In twilight the lamp illumines ideological will
A weaving of walls, movable wicker
& caravan carpets strung twixt reeds
Our ground breathes, floats, as we wander
Into cosmologies, cosmogonies
Immeasurable emblems of circumference or protractor

3.

She developed the disease of demonic enthusiasm
On looking at a nymph,
Mystic hunt through childhood, *histoire* of fountains
Dominating the *jardin*   canary parasols
Perpetual noon   antipasto sun   *crème* ballerina
Idyllic dying swan

4.

Wire-netted cage papered with constellations
Promises of progress or unfoldment from her magic prison [torso]
She traces an analemma, her eyes infinitely distant,
Maps night sky or soap bubbles
Navigated by songbird
Whose droppings streak the air
Reminiscent for us of a comet's tail
The result of yesterday's path-strewn bird crumbs

5.

Occupants of the *Etrangers*
Exalted chanters with a self-contained view
Small white frame
Moon
Sustained patterns of meaning

Spindly-armed shadows stretch through lace curtains
Historians of the mind's voyage

As with other repressions, a vestige of the animal within
Seamless continuum, therefore the bordertown Nostalgia

Her liquid limbs, she interior
To the melody alone

Unraveled eveners

Foaming grottoes & feathered
Lures — yearnings of detachment
Symbolized and effected

Travelogue of a faun's dream

THE APPEARANCE OF THINGS
Dale Peck

YOU WONDERED WHY he chose to build something like this. Before that, actually, you wondered why he chose to build it here. Was build the right word? Perhaps construct would have been better, or situate; but still, why did he make his home *here*? When you got off the train you wrapped your scarf around your throat. Yes, you told yourself, double-checking J.'s directions, you'd gotten off at the right place. A few streetlights stabbed at the darkness, casting long shadows on the buildings that surrounded you. Tall buildings, emptied tenements with crumbling cinderblocks filling in their windows. The rain-washed remains of wheat-pasted posters filled in those boxes with strange stories involving cigarettes and alcohol and coffee and birds, and the glass that had once filled the same holes crunched beneath your feet. You told yourself you'd walked through the looking-glass, but when you chuckled aloud at your attempt at a joke the sound dissipated into the abandoned evening and you shivered a little, turned up your collar, thrust your hands in your pockets and started walking. Three children played inside the glowing cone cast by a corner streetlight. Shadows made their clothes—was that velvet? lace?—look like some kind of antique costume, and the white marbles they rolled across the sidewalk seemed to be elongated white spheres that wobbled erratically when flicked by finger or thumb. Seeing you, the trio grew silent and stared as you passed, recognizing you as the stranger you were; when you were ten paces beyond them the clicks of their egg-shaped marbles against each other signaled their return to the game. Still later, there was a low voiceless voice from a recess in a building, Hey, yo, check it out, you heard, and when you didn't respond to the voice you heard a wheezing laugh and the brief scrape of a boot across the glass-strewn sidewalk. Two coins bounced out of the black behind you, and when you stopped to pick them up your foot caught in a fissure in the sidewalk; a glow appeared, pulsed, then faded away. You jerked your foot free, dropped the coins in your pocket, and jogged to the next streetlight, where you read J.'s instructions again. When you finally found his building, you paused for a moment. A newspaper blew past you, screaming fire and famine, and then it was gone. J.'s building, seven stories tall, was another tenement. The windows of its first six floors were filled with cinderblocks, those on the top floor with glass and darkness. The lock grudgingly received the key you slid from his envelope, and then the metal door opened silently. The light inside, as out, was sparse, and every ten steps your shadow stretched in front of you, longer and fainter, until it was gone for another ten steps and then reappeared. The elevator shaft, you'd learned from his letter, lay at the end of the hallway. The door stood already open—only one elevator, and it was on the building's ground floor. You rode in silence to the seventh floor, leaning against the side of the box, smelling, faintly, wood. The paint, you noticed then, had been stripped from the elevator car's walls, and in the thin light inside the car the residue of color could have been maroon or simply brown. You pressed your nose against the cool wood and inhaled deeply. Pine, you thought. Cedar. Certainly it was neither of those, but since you didn't know the scent of any other wood from memory you had to generalize from your experience, and when the elevator door opened at the seventh floor you inhaled once more before leaving. Does rose-wood smell like roses? Seventy feet above the ground (there, you told yourself, that is a fact, that is indisputable—but then it occurred to you that the building might have a basement) you retraveled the hall-way which had led you from the street. Almost at its end—a paned window whose glass had been covered in paper—you came to a door, 701, his door, J.'s, and it was ajar. You pushed then, pushed it slowly because an unlocked door seemed to you an odd thing. "J.?" you called; but the only answer was your echoed voice: *Jay, Jay*. Inside, at last, light. Bright but not overpowering, soft but still odd. The light shone from under the couch, behind an empty vase, its glow reminis-cent of the sun's after it's slipped below the horizon. The effect was of sourcelessness and you took in everything it illuminated in that long narrow room: the earthy seams of the wooden floor, a strip of green carpet; the couches and chairs upholstered in fabric the color and tex-ture of cattails; the bare brownish walls; the blue ceiling. The room tried for an effect, you weren't sure what, nor if it succeeded, but as you walked its length you were reminded of a phrase from one of J.'s letters, *the world is just a box*, and you traveled the length of the room, at one point catching the tip of your shoe on the carpet's edge and nearly falling. Down there (where he told you it would) the door to J.'s bedroom waited, closed. J., you thought, J. must be in there. Opening it, you immediately slipped on the sand that covered the floor. Nearly an inch deep, the dry grains emerged from under the desk, the dresser, the two night tables, the bed, as though the sand, like the leafy shag in the living room, were just another carpet. J. wasn't in the neat room. On his desk, though, you saw a tiny box made of wire mesh, a little wider than your hand, half as deep, crammed with paper. The sand crunched under your feet as you crossed the room; even before you reached the box you recognized the paper as the letters you had returned to him at his request, the many letters that had become his epistle, the epistle that became his parable, the parable that became, finally, his story. (The words are J.'s, and appear fre-quently in that thing. But if it is a story, it's a story without dialogue;

you must imagine what's being said.) Only the first letter remained in its envelope; the rest were loose in the chest. You knew from having read and reread them all many times that two hundred and ninety-seven pages resided there, and you knew also, without taking the very first letter from its yellowed envelope, what its first line reads: *It's not enough, it's never enough, merely to understand.* It's not enough, it's never enough. He wrote it twice: he wanted you to understand him. Quickly you placed the first letter in your overcoat pocket. Its presence noisily disturbed the two coins you'd forgotten about, and you noticed then that you were still bundled for outside. You loosened the coat's belt, undid the buttons, unwrapped your scarf. Leaving the letter with directions to J.'s house in your coat, you moved the older letter and the coins to your pants pocket, then took off the coat and scarf and laid them across the smooth green spread that covered J.'s bed. A sound, like wind, came from beyond the second door, which stood outlined in light at the far end of the room. You ignored the wind—you didn't understand its language yet—and instead allowed yourself to wonder once again why J. chose to create an apartment like this. But that question, besides being unanswerable, raised so many other questions that all you decided to go to the second door after all, a little quickly even, you trotted to the door and pushed through it and tripped over a sand drift and your falling weight sends you crashing into a blinding flash of sunlight. You're blind for a long time, laying there with sand in your mouth, hands over your eyes. Sweat trickles from beneath your pressed-together fingers before you take them away. Standing up, looking around you, you lick your fingers dry. A desert lies beyond J.'s second door, a vast desert, so large that the sand curves up at the horizon and seems to close over itself like the reflected lid of a casket lined with golden cloth. But your first step into this desert lands not on sand but on a gray cinderblock, and then, as you watch, the stirring wind uncovers a serpentine cement path stretching into the desert. Can you walk its length? You don't know. You notice the clothes you chose for this meeting: your pants, whose dark delicate fabric has been ripped by your fall; your shirt; a pair of thin black leather loafers through which you already feel the path's heat as you step, and step again, and step again. Your clothes were ill-suited for the winter you started out in but they're even more out of place here; still, you ignore that, and instead you concentrate on placing one foot in front of another on the path and you tell yourself that what you are doing is walking. You are walking through the desert that lies beyond J.'s door, and somewhere in your mind there is the tacit understanding that it is a finite desert because J. lived in an area dense with buildings, so sooner or later you should hit another one. But because you left J.'s instructions in your coat which remains on his bed you're not sure. J. You turn to see how far you've walked from his room. Then you start to run. When you've run a long time without seeing anything but sand and the wasted hulls of plants and here and there huge corks the size of buoys, as if the casks they'd once stoppered had been the size of barrels, you notice that the path under your feet has begun booming hollowly with each footfall. The corks and the plants speak of some past gardener's efforts, but where, you wonder, is the gardener, where did he get his water? But there's nothing you can do about that, so you keep running on the hollow path until eventually the desert slopes away beneath your feet, gradually, not suddenly, it forms a ravine, a pit almost, whose far side is so steep and slippery with sand that you fall twice as you scale it, first time ripping your right pant leg, second time skinning your left elbow. Over the hill is still the desert, but not only the desert. There, directly before you, though several steps away, stands a tree. The path takes you almost to it, then veers sharply to the left. Though it's right there, you can't make out any of its feathers. *Features*, you mean, but feathers seems an understandable slip, because much of the tree is obscured by a downy layer of white leaves that are long and tapered and folded over lengthwise, like the feathers on the ruff of a crested cockatoo or the wings of a paper airplane. No, no, that's too much: there is nothing about this tree except itself and the words printed on each leaf which move about too quickly for you to read, and you are afraid to touch it, to grab a feather and hold it still so you can focus on its message. Instead you circle it, and a quarter of the way around the tree your foot accidentally leaves the path for the first time. The sand pulls softly on your foot; it's hot, but cooler than the reflected heat of the cement. It's scratchy though, inside your shoes, and you take them off. Three steps have you directly under the tree. Those white leaves cast no shade, no shadows. The trunk rises from the ground in a single column (there is that flare at the bottom; for a moment you see inside yourself, into your own darkness, roots reaching underground, connecting with miles of soil below the sand, with water too, and other trees). The trunk gives way to three branches which twist about each other once before going their separate ways. Did you notice that the bark is pearly white? Like ash, you think, or aspen, or perhaps a very young elm. Again you're limited by your experience; this tree is neither ash nor aspen nor elm, nor is it like them, but your experience, your memory, is all you have to go on. The three primary branches each give way to three more branches and these to three more. You go through and count them all again to make sure you haven't misread: yes, there are three and three and three each, but the effect isn't of some dull masonry-like order because the secondary and tertiary branches take their time appearing and don't rush anywhere, coiling slowly out and about before digressing, finally, into three more branches each. It's from these final branches that the willowy white-leaved lines hang. But not just hang, you notice, for they swirl around each other in pairs and triples and more, loop back to curl around the larger branches, or hang loosely in the air. But this is all you can understand without touching the tree; this is all you can see. You try to read the words on the leaves again, but you can't. The leaves are too far away and twist out of your vision, and yet you know they are words; you just don't know what they say. You sniff, smelling for a floral or a woody scent; there is none. You cock your ears, listening for a rustle of leaves in the wind that might tell you something; but there is neither wind nor words, except for those printed on the leaves, which you could read if you pulled a branch closer to you. You reach out a hand, then pull it back, then take several steps backward, your feet digging in the loose

sand. The tree remains, only three or four times taller than you, bal-
anced like a black and white fountain on a slender column. From such
a tree you would not be surprised if a serpent descended to speak to
you in its seductive whisper, or if a parrot perched among its branches
to riddle you with repeated words. Some thought like this is in your
head anyway, and even as it bats around your brain the tree shudders
once, twice, a third time, and then all of its leaves fall from it in a body,
into a body: the leaves are assuming some kind of shape, but before
they can coalesce into some new creature to menace you, you turn and
run again, your bare feet burning with every step, your head hanging,
your tongue dry and swollen in your mouth, your eyes on the sun-
baked earth which booms hollowly with each footfall, and creaks as
well, and threatens to crack beneath your weight. You can feel blisters
form on your feet, feel also the skin on the back of your neck burn in
the harsh light. When you scratch it, the skin flakes away in white
scales like the leaves falling—no, you remind yourself. Like skin.
Simply skin. Sunburned skin flaking away under scratching fingers.
Watching the flakes drift to the ground, you stub your toe on a step.
You look back and see that the ground you trod has collapsed in on
itself and the resulting chasm is sucking up all the hot light from the
desert. Then you turn and see a tall staircase, not immensely tall but
a good deal taller than you, running up the side of a high wall. You
can't see the top landing actually, because a lamp hanging from a pole
stuck in the wall snaps on in the falling light, burning so brightly that
it blinds you and again you close your eyes. You reach out with your
left hand and remember, as the loosely formed scab splits, your
skinned elbow. With a wince you grab the banister; eyes closed, you
take a step, and then another, and then another. You keep your eyes
closed until the lamp's heat is behind you. When you open them the
glare is gone; the earth has consumed the excess light like a sunset,
restoring harmony, and the grassy plain stretching out before you has
only a naked man to interrupt its surface. Because you notice that he's
naked, the first part of him you see is his cock, soft and white against
the bottom part of his belly. He's hairless, you notice then, except for

his head, covered in bleach-white strands which mix with the shadowy grass he's laid in. His eyes are open and he's not breathing. Is this, finally, J.? It might as well be. Is he dead? What does that mean? You find in your pocket the coins you found a long time ago and take them out. A bigger one, a smaller one. (The adjectives are comparative, I know, but they're all we have to go on here. Is the one big as coins go, the other small? You don't know.) Using the edge of the coins, you push the man's eyelids closed. His eyeballs recede in their sockets under the pressure. First the bigger coin, then the smaller; with that one you can't help but touch his skin. It's warm, porous; there's sweat on your finger and his skin seems to absorb it. Then, his eyes closed and held shut by the coins, you look at him again. But what is there to see that you haven't seen before? No, looking at him isn't enough, and suddenly, without thinking, you run your hand over his box, his *body* you mean, you let your fingers trail down the smooth expanse of his stomach, flicking aside the cock when you get there and traveling down his right leg. The skin at his knee is no harder than the rest of his skin, as though he's worn clothes all his life, never had occasion to cut his knees on a gritty road after falling, never stood too long on bare cement. He's so warm, almost hot! Though the body itself invites interpretation, you can find no answer to your question: what happened to this man? You can find no answer to any of your questions, but everything, you are forced to admit, has made its own strange sense. Everything was as J. said it would be in his directions, or at least as far as you followed them. The progression from one step to the next has been clear and logical, and if this final destination seems at an unexpectedly great remove from your journey's starting point—if indeed this man is your destination—well, you still don't feel *lost*. Confused, maybe, and tired. God, you're exhausted, as if you and not J. have gone to all this effort to stuff the world into a box. You step back suddenly; the smaller coin has proved too light to hold the man's eye closed and his right lid snaps open, tossing the coin in the grass where it disappears, but even as you step back you think maybe it was you. Maybe *you* put everything there; maybe you threw it away. The man still doesn't move though, still doesn't breathe, but you take another step back, as much to escape the sight of the silver coin as the gaze of his single open eye. Understand something quickly: he's not looking at you, and even if he were, his vision alone can't affect you. Do you understand that? You must, because the wind is blowing now and licking at your ears. You feel it tell you goodbye; is it, perhaps, speaking for the man, the man you call J., who rolls now, rolls over in the wind? He rolls once, then again, and then again, taking with him the strip of grass that he passes over. It grows larger and larger as he blow-rolls away from you and you look at it and think, inside that core of earth and grass is a man you have touched with your hand. You look at your hand, spread the fingers, see between them the pale glint of water. Where the man and the grass were, there is now a long dark strip of clear water. You have choices again: you can go to that water, or go instead to that bowl there, a wide, circular, nearly flat basin enameled blue and painted with a black pattern (things just appear in this world, you've noticed that; given time, anything might happen). The basin is filled with water too. You could go to it, drink from it like a horse, clearing it of silt with one breath, sucking in water with the next, or you could raise its awkward shape to your lips and drink sloppily, spilling water all over your chafed skin. Or you could remove your clothes like you're doing now and—you're way ahead of me, you're diving into the river created by the man's rolling body. (You don't see the one drop of water from your splash that makes ripples in the painted basin, but that's okay: you understand enough already.) You wonder briefly why you brought J.'s letter all this way only to abandon it in his closet, but that thought is interrupted, then erased, by the prickly sensation of water mixing with blood in your elbow. You grab and turn the handle at the bottom of the spring—pool? river? the difference between words is enormous, but inconsequential as well—and then you're washed in a flood onto J.'s bed, and after the roar of rushing water subsides you hear a coin plink once, twice, and then a third time on a floor washed clean of sand, and then the feathers start falling. Thousands of them, like warm flakes of snow, sticking to your wet skin and giving you not wings but…what? Perhaps J. will know the word you need. Perhaps it's not a word you're looking for (and you close your eyes then, lest you see them written on the feathers, on your body). It's as if you've looked all the way through J.'s world to a mirror at the back of it, a mirror in which you are surprised to find yourself, and you suddenly understand that though you can go left or right in this world you can't go wrong. You can go forward or back but you can't leave anything behind. You think then that each new thing that's appeared here has been an admission that apocalypse exists even as it was staved off a little longer. Esoteric creation is just a parody of annihilation, a joke at death's expense, and when you finally see that J.'s included *you* in that frame your choices seem neither limited nor, more to the point, fraught with something so limiting as meaning. New words come to you, words like connection, exclusion, relationship; the word object serves only as a reminder of the world's flux, and all you can do, really, is wait. So: wait. For J.'s appearance, or his continued absence, or some other miracle. Because waiting, after all, is just a way of letting the world come to you.

SLIDE SHOW

Joanna Scott

ONCE WE'RE SETTLED and I've figured out how to work this machine, the switch here, that's it, now if you could dim the lights, Mrs. Dewitt, yes, completely, and shut the door. All right then.

I've been invited to speak to your society today about birds and their attributes. We'll begin with the Troglodyte genus, *T. Fulvus*, the common house wren. Brown, banded with dusky gray, length about 4 inches. To quote the Honorable S. G. Goodrich, "The species has a very merry, rollicking song, and displays great antipathy to cats, especially those which venture near their nests."

It's useful, don't you think, to take a good long look at a familiar species from time to time?

No, Mr. Cornell, the negative is not for sale.

Onward. Here we have—

You're absolutely right, Mrs. Dewitt. This is not a bird. This is a representative of the *Homo sapiens* species, circa 1920. Otherwise known as Maria B, native of Wethersfield, Connecticut. A common housewife. Note the sling. Mrs. B's right arm is in a cast up to the elbow. Mrs. B isn't smiling. Mrs. B, generally humorless, could usually be counted upon to smile for photographs. But for this photograph Mrs. B had no reason to smile because Mrs. B had a broken arm.

Yes, Mr. Flaherty, I took this photograph.

No, Mrs. Dewitt, I am not wandering from my topic. If you'll bear with me.

There, no, wrong way. Here we go, one more, all right then. The nest of a wren with seven peach-colored eggs. Note how the eggs are sprinkled evenly with purplish flecks. If you look closely you'll notice that the feathers lining the nest are not only wren. There is evidence of sparrows, martins, a robin. This is characteristic of the nest of *T. Fulvus*.

Which brings me to my first word of advice for you birders: Never disturb a wren's nest, not even if *T. Fulvus* builds it in the pocket of your raincoat, as she's been known to do. Let me repeat: Never disturb a wren's nest. Remember this. Mrs. B forgot, or else she was never warned. My neighbor, Mrs. B of Wethersfield—let me go back, no, wrong way, back again, one more, here we are—Mrs. B, my neighbor in Wethersfield, ripped a nest from the cornice under the eaves of her house one fine May morning because she could not stand to be woken by the singing of the wrens, and in June she fell off a ladder and broke her arm.

No, Mrs. Kemp, I wasn't there when she broke her arm. I was away at college at the time. What? Harvard. What? Yes, thank you.

Next we move on to *P. Cristatus*. The peafowl, tinted blue and golden-green, with his long, glittering tail, the feathers bejeweled with eye-spots. The proud, prancing, polygamous peacock, native to India but naturalized as a domestic bird around the world.

Who in the audience would be willing to demonstrate the shriek of a peacock? Mrs. Kemp? Go ahead, Mrs. Kemp.

Well done, Mrs. Kemp.

Next we'll turn to . . . to . . . to the Peacocks, Atlantic City, New Jersey, 1935. A capella singers. Do they look like birds, Mrs. Dewitt? If you'll bear with me? Thank you. Is there anyone present who ever had the good fortune to hear this group? No? "They sing like angels"—this was the pronouncement of Bing Crosby after hearing The Peacocks at a club in New York in the winter of 1935. The endorsement should have been the beginning of their rise. Instead it was the peak before their steep decline. Why was it they sang like angels one day, and the next day they couldn't sing on key? Why was it they were all the rage in 1935, and a year later they were out of work?

Yes, Mr. Flaherty, I saw them on several occasions.

No, Mr. Cornell, I did not get their autographs.

Here we have the Peacocks on stage at a county fair, Midland, Illinois, 1936—one of their last performances. If you look carefully, you'll see that each one has a peacock feather strapped to his leg— courtesy of Bing. Angels must have feathers, he insisted, and the next day he had a box of peacock plumage sent over to the hotel where the singers were staying. Beginning in the winter of 1935, the Peacocks wore peacock feathers whenever they performed. Each with a pea-cock feather strapped to his right leg—their trademark and their curse.

Hence my second point to emphasize: If you must collect pea-cock feathers, do not bring them onto a stage.

Yes, Mr. Flaherty, I took this photograph.

No, Mr. Cornell, I do not have a peacock feather of my own.

All right then, we'll move on to the Corvidae. *Corvus americanus*. The common crow. Color a glossy blue-black, seventeen inches in length. A vagabond, a pest, he is trapped in clap-nets, poisoned by farmers, shot by bounty hunters. But still he persists, enabled by his extreme intelligence. I knew a man who found a fledgling crow, took it home, and kept it as a pet. Let me show you—

Mr. Z, of Meridian, Massachusetts, 1927. Yes, another *Homo sapien*, Mrs. Dewitt—Mr. Z with his pet crow, Rook, on his shoulder, the first crow of six kept by Mr. Z. Rook learned to open the latch of the front gate for Mr. Z when he came home from work. He'd fly at strangers, screaming in fury, until Mr. Z called him off. Soon even Mr. Z's friends stopped visiting. Then Mr. Z lost his job. The following week a tree fell on his house during a storm. He grew progressively weaker and became prone to dizzy spells. He stirred the smelling salts into his soup. He put his shoes on the wrong feet and wore his wristwatch upside down.

Everything was going to ruin for Mr. Z.

You see before you Magpie, Mr. Z's second pet crow. Magpie appeared out of nowhere one day. She sat hunched on Mr. Z's fence all morning long, and eventually Rook flew over and hunched beside her, and after that the two crows were inseparable.

Here again is Mr. Z—the same Mr. Z, prospering, as you can see. He'd found another job, a better job, in a local drugstore. Also employed at the drugstore was the young widow who would turn out to be his future wife. Though he was still sickly, things were looking up for Mr. Z.

Here, next, the Dainty Maw, Mr. Z's third crow. This one he purchased from a migrant worker who had kept the crow on a leash day and night. The crow, with nothing to eat but rotten windapples and the occasional scrap of sandwich thrown to him by his owner, was ailing. Mr. Z paid two dollars for him. It took just one week on a proper diet for the crow to be restored to health.

As the health of the Dainty Maw improved, so too did Mr. Z's health. He regained his balance, his energy, his appetite. He put on weight. His hair thickened. He married the widow on a brisk fall day.

Next we have Mr. Z's Corby, his fourth *Corvus americanus*, who was lured from a nearby rookery by the chattering of Magpie. Corby is a beautiful specimen, as you can see—tinted with a purplish gloss, long-winged, with a crest on his forehead, as though he had a bit of the jay in him. He was as arrogant as a jay and took every opportunity to peck the others, especially after he learned that Magpie was unavailable.

Here are Mr. and Mrs. Z circa 1928, proud comanagers of a Liggett Rexalls. Notice the string of pearls Mrs. Z is wearing. Notice the ring on her left hand.

But now the story of Mr. Z takes another turn, with the arrival of crows number five and six, Hood and Gor, a morose pair who abandoned their own flock but never wanted much to do with the crows of Mr. Z. Here you see them on Mr. Z's roof, perched on the edge of the gutter, lazily watching the world go by. Day and night, month after month, they watched. They watched Mr. and Mrs. Z walk up the road toward town each day. They watched Mr. Z push his mower around the yard. They watched Mr. Z grow thin and weak. They watched Rook fly at the doctor when he came up the front walk. They watched Rook fly at the doctor when he left. They watched Mr. Z carried away in coffin. They watched the snow fall. They watched Mrs. Z come out of the house alone. She paused, waiting for Rook to unlatch the front gate. She slipped on the icy sidewalk but caught herself and stayed upright. She turned, looked up at Hood and Gor, and shook her fist at them. Why? she thought. Why was she a widow again? Why?

Which leads me to my final piece of wisdom for the evening: If you're going to keep crows, remember that one crow is bad, two's luck, three's health, four's wealth, five's sickness, and six is death.

So there you have it, ladies and gentlemen—an introduction to some of the more influential attributes of birds. With more time I would have considered the owl, the starling, the seagull, maybe even the titmouse. Perhaps we'll have another occasion. At any rate, to review quickly the material we've covered in today's lecture: Destroy a wren's nest and you'll break a bone within the year. A peacock feather on stage will bring misfortune. And how many crows bring health?

Brilliant, Miss...Miss? Miss Lucas!

The point, Mrs. Dewitt? Why the point is, we must pay attention to the birds! Not just cast a glance in order to make an identification, but really notice them. Their habits and moods and skills and histories. Their feather barbs and powder down, their reptilian feet and horny sheathed beaks. Their black spinel eyes that see everything. Their call-notes, their clattering and fluttering. Pit-wit, pit-wit, cries the sandpiper. Chip-chip-chip, trills the chipping sparrow. The twilight song of the wood pewee. The dawn song of the kingbird. What are they trying to tell us? What have we overlooked? We give them names and classification, we map their migratory paths, we organize the information, and then we go home to dinner. But information is worthless without the exaltation of experience. There is more to learn from the world than simple facts. We must take our time to notice, really notice, what we're looking at. If we paid attention to the birds, we would see what's coming!

Mrs. Dewitt, the lights, please. I thank you all for listening. It's been a pleas—

Summa cum laude, Mrs. Kemp.

Yes, Mr. Flaherty, I call myself a scientist.

No, Mr. Cornell, not a single one of my negatives is for sale. Good night.

BIRDS OF A FEATHER

Diane Ackerman

Abracadabra, and birds fly.
Meaty yet ghostlike, they change shape
to pirouette on high, casting daggers
of glare or broad black shadows.
To the devout, flying crucifixions.
Sitting nearly motionless on a limb,
they continue flying, but at zero speed,
as the wind soughs through them.
Even their fallen feathers fly.

Like shamans or courtiers,
they rehearse the intricate rituals
and ceremonies that rule lives.
A courting crow on the outs
performs an appeasement gesture,
dropping a succulent berry
at a glossy female's feet.
She stops chattering abuse,
edges closer, burbles, rolls a rebus eye.
Another male stages his own
private one-bird vaudeville show
with hopscotch, tap dance,
acrobatics, trendy tunes.

Aloft, birds look like parts of sky
that have broken loose.
Alternately angelic and stark,
they slide across the blue on wings
softer than skin, soft as our gold standard
for softness, while constantly
opening and closing an array
of small doors in their wings
(closed with each downflap,
cupping the air, then open on upflaps
so air can stream through). Masters
of silent commotion, do they hear,
feel door feathers slamming shut?

In wistfulness and envy, I gaze at them,
lamenting just how earthbound I live,
and sigh the poignant subjunctive
of our species: *If only.* If only
I could beguile the winds, if only
I could float the sky upon my shoulders.

BOOKMARK, HORIZON
(EMILY DICKINSON)
Ann Lauterbach

Where whatever the *blue* was
found its hesitancy as pierced inscription
           drew dispersal

back through the sieve towards the eye's
singular vantage

        face of a girl
           and the first room on the top floor
             1425

    the glossed immersion
    as if a jar could open space

        aught in the old vitrine
    thwart of song
    thwart the incipience of cloud, and the leftover, omitted arc
           a rig for flight

which might have been a habit of scale
or the fast stopped by your gaze

        what stalled? the glassy circumference?
        the dainty primer of decay? inquisitive ink drained from sound?

the room enlarged beyond fog, beyond the bending annotated way
unbound by its wall, where *l'etoile*
           is embossed on the stationery
           and the sign is dry —

                        turn, swift bearer, brief
volition, at the far, the furthest, shore.

Because I Could Not Stop For Death

Mary Caponegro

How soft this Prison is
How sweet these sullen bars

? / ? / ?

Some might call the white light harsh, so bright is it, but I find
comfort in its angular embrace; it calls to mind an Amherst winter
(despite the former's angles and the latter's curving hills), during
which one, if troubled of mind, could walk and not be seen, hidden by
the snow's silence, or perch at an upstairs window writing (as I
increasingly might do instead of walking), writing words that could as
well be blanketed by the white page...

*A woman carefully placing the nib of her pen in an inkwell, transfer-
ring it to a white rectangular surface, making marks in a hand slanted
far to the right, then taking the same pen and putting a line through
some of the marks she has made.*

...Now I perch inside this sweet if stark white cell you, connoisseur of confection, shaped for me of empathy and imagination, and carry out the correspondence you requested of me. How could I not comply, having made so many such entreaties while I was alive? Who would have thought that through my parceled words and your ingenious spiritual rectangle, there could be communication of this sort? I once joked with a dear friend that the correspondence he and I sustained felt like writing notes *to* the sky, as his replies were scanter than my letters to him. Wouldn't he be amused to see that I now write notes *from* the sky?

A man lovingly fingering a photograph in a shop crowded with bric-a-brac, then moving his hand to the brittle, yellowed leaves of a book.

Dear Miss Emily,

The receipt of your letter, coming as it did through idiosyncratic postal means, was timed magnificently with a lifting of several days of oppressive humidity. Your words move me very much (as they always have in other forms). I am deeply honored by your correspondence, and your visit, which believe it or not was as much a surprise to me as to you. When I constructed the box, Miss Emily, I did not mean for it to disrupt you in any way; I repeat, I only meant to pay you tribute. An artist, it is said, manipulates his world, but I would never dream of manipulating you.

A woman with a newspaper spread before her, rotating it slowly on the table, one quarter-turn to the left, meticulously filling its margins with additional lines of sharply angled letters from her own pen; then, when there is no more white space remaining, supplementing these margins with the backs of envelopes and scraps of paper.

A man meticulously collating small objects, labeling the fronts of file boxes, then writing across the entire width of a brown paper bag, line by line, until he has filled it from top to bottom.

Having grown quite settled in my spirit-cell, how strange it was when the entire edifice somehow tipped on its side, causing me to spin around several times, as the perch became a round seat atop a sturdy metal cylinder jutting out of the floor, and you to whom I had not yet been introduced sat beside me on another exactly its twin, both of us facing a high table, behind which stood a scantily-clad serving girl and an aproned man in full view, cooking. And my blue sky's window expanded into a window far larger in dimension and far less aesthetically pleasing in its contents. This occurred, I can only surmise, because you summoned me, Mr. Cornell, although even after the fact you remain quite cagy about the matter. I would have thought the episode a dream had I not surrendered the practice of dreaming when I exited life.

A boy in a crowd, wide-eyed, watching a man on a stage extricating himself from chains, emerging from inside a locked vault.

The episode was enough to give one nervous collapse—all over again!—although in a sense it was the opposite of the darkness I first assumed had been my death when I fainted in the kitchen baking. This incident was more like fainting *into* light—a different, a benign kind of Bright's disease, you might say.

It was certainly enough to make one marvel, and I continue to ponder it here within the structure I have come to call my rectangle of reflection.

10 / 3

yesterday met Miss Emily—out of the blue, you might say—there she was at Bick's. persuaded her after to come to Utopia Parkway to see the work (after initial tentativity she assented; in fact, insisted). in Bick's she was very suspicious of the fare, dismayed at how I reveled in it, but later let me take her to Shelley's, too, and the automat—we talked a lot—told me her brother's nickname: "his highness." told her mine: Choey by my sisters—Boysey by father. and mentioned Robert.

that was only the beginning of the many words exchanged. much shared.

> We talked with each other about each other
> Though neither of us spoke–

I beg your pardon, sir. Would you be so kind as to inform me where I am?

With pleasure, Madam. A diner called Bickford's. A county called Queens.

I have been to Washington, to Boston, and to Philadelphia, but never to a place called Queens. And who are you, if I am not too bold?

Will it be the usual, Mr. Cornell? Or should I say, *which* usual? Oh, pardon, didn't see the lady. Hey, what is this, a costume party?

Consider yourself indirectly introduced, Mr. Cornell.

Need I ask to whom?

Who am I, but a woman in white, who was heard but not seen, who had no mother, then discovered she did, who walked with her dog and sat with her cat, who had a way with flowers, whose father would eat only her bread, whose Indian rye won a prize, who made more than adequate pudding, who did not care to clean or sew, who hoarded her words for the bureau drawer but barely aired them in the light of day. Don't you know yet who I am?

What can I order for you, Miss Emily?

I haven't eaten in so many years; I imbibe the white light of the blue peninsula. I believe you saw to that, Mr. Cornell—arranged for my sustenance.

It's questions I long to feed you, Miss Emily—hundreds of them.

One banana cream pie, extra whipped.

Do you long for life, Miss Emily?

I admire a man who does not traffic in small talk. If I am not too cryptic, I longed more for the first phase of life during life than I now long for life in the afterlife.

You are not at all cryptic. But maybe you could solve me a riddle or two. For example, Miss Emily, how is it that your Amherst winter blossoms into my Indian summer?—I, who was born on Christmas Eve but find my understanding of you coalesces in that skewed autumn season's sensibility.

I have fewer clues than you, Mr. Cornell, who are, it appears, the inadvertent author of my afterlife—despite my life having preceded yours! Now that is a paradox more than ripe for poem—but death interrupted the practice.

Of penning, you mean?

Yes. Penning. Poem-ing? Time, one might say, stopped, but that is not entirely accurate; rather, time passes now so differently than in my life—or former life—when we could chart the seasons by consistent reliable signs; when mother came back from walking with a burdock clinging to her shawl, for instance, we celebrated spring—until, of course, the day that mother ceased to walk outside, or walk at all, those seven years.

I understand, Miss Emily, I understand. My brother was, all his years, more or less immobile.

Who cared for him?

I did, mainly.

A brother is the fulcrum of a family.

Yes. Please go on.

Brothers leaven our lives with their playful humor. Mothers, on the other hand, sober one's life with their needs—as is appropriate, for too much liveliness would not be proper; excess animation would lend a wildness unsuitable to domestic life.

We are in sync, Miss Emily. I'll confess that when I first thought of you, because I felt so connected to you, I hoped you had a sweet tooth and your brother a handicap.

You are a peculiar man, in more ways than one. Albeit a greatly gifted one. My intuition tells me one of your gifts might be gardening. Do you possess a garden, Mr. Cornell?

Indeed I do, Miss E—a very special one, if small. One with quince tree and birdbath and rabbit.

A woman gathering fruit from a garden, first carefully, then in a frenzy —shaking the trees, until the abundance of their yield overwhelms her: a deluge of apples, peaches, and figs, gathered up in her skirt, nearly burying her—her head and shoulders bobbing above the smaller round objects, until she emerges, steadies herself, and starts to walk, then run, racing after the mail coach with all she can carry of them: "Please, coachman, bring these to Austin with love from his sister!"

Or bore the Garden in the Brain
This Curiosity—

Once I scolded my brother for poaching poetry—his highness had enough accomplishments without usurping mine—but I also scorned his wife for displaying one of my poems. I realize it may seem contradictory. You, I sense, are at home with paradox, Mr. Cornell, as, thanks to your antics, I've thoroughly lost track of how many times I died before I died!

10 / 4

weather today in fact a misty quality similar to that spectre—scrumptious Debussy Preludes by Gieseking augment this feeling—hope I did not insult E.D. when I said I preferred the cupcake to her hand-picked figs. good find in Strand. special treat for Robert too. Mother keeps asking, Who was the polite young woman? I approve of her. will she come again? and that I should bring home proper young ladies like E all the time.

A woman playing the piano, intent, rapturous.

A boy holding his younger sister's hand, listening with delight as his mother plays the piano and his father sings.

? / ? / ?

On my honor, Joseph, I shall continue to answer the questions which you have kept, as you say, in storage. I know I have yet to address your positioning of life in opposition to aesthetics—I am still trying to understand it fully. And I could not explain in any logical terms how I recognized you almost immediately as my spiritual architect, shall we say—as if your face matched a photograph I'd looked at all my afterlife. But here is the answer to a question you did not ask me: Were I to make a box for you—had I your unusual gifts and could return the favor, that is—it would consist of the following: quince petals and sugar cubes—the former in opulent heaps, the latter in stacks.

10 / 5

the visitation of E.D. is truly a marvelous thing—even more so than seeing Mary Baker Eddy on the park bench that day, but must consider implications for current and future boxes. perhaps this is the solution to the malady of being trapped in boxes—that they have the capacity to liberate others.

A man bowing his head in prayer.

A woman doing the same.

My question, Mr. Cornell—for you must allow me a question or two, though perhaps you do not know the answer yourself—concerning The Blue Peninsula: Is this the final destination or an intermediate stage of my eternity?

A boy fervently lining up miniature cakes on a shelf, examining each one as if it were a jewel, inhaling its aroma with eyes closed.

And while you formulate that answer, a simpler question: Is it salubrious, Mr. Cornell, to have dessert before the main course?

But it *is* the main course, Miss Emily, dessert is always the main course! And we shall have more of it at our next stop: the bakery. Nothing could be more essential!

A man doubled over in pain on a park bench, clutching his stomach.

A woman bending over an invalid, supporting her, raising her torso until she sits up in the bed, then sitting beside her and spooning food from a bowl into her mouth.

A man helping a younger man out of bed, giving him ballast with his body.

How could you refuse a Seckel pear, Mr Cornell? Tell me, when you sit beneath your quince tree in the theatre of nature do you nibble at a bar of candy?

In fact, I often do; my favorite is the Milky Way.

The milky way?

It marries chocolate to the heavens and that, to me, Miss Emily, is a very favorable marriage indeed. The best of both worlds, you might say.

A boy closing a book and opening a window to look up at the stars, then huddling under the covers of his bed, trembling.

After all Birds have been investigated and laid aside

?/?/?
Dear friend,

You needn't have apologized for the condition of your workspace. I am not fastidious in that respect. After all, a writer need only deal with clutter of the mind, and paper even in accumulation stacks quite neatly. The source of the distress you sensed was something else: the house you had spoken of earlier, with brass and oak and French doors, and the boats on the Hudson River visible from the porch—that was where I thought you were taking me to view your artwork. I felt close to my own memories of Amherst when you rhapsodized about it. This childhood was no fiction, was it? With homemade preserves hidden inside one of two pianos on Christmas morning? (We had only one piano in our mansion, but I could match you if you count my piano in the woods.)

But I want to speak of your current studio. Peering in upon those birds and stars and shells and such, the plethora of curious artifacts, Joseph, I felt I had been to church. I once said to a dear friend (the same to whom I joked about skywriting) that he was my church. But here in this case it is not a human heart and mind's embrace that offers surrogate worship, but a man-made miniature environment, diminutive, such as only a doll could comfortably enter—yet my entire consciousness now loiters in such a one with impunity—luxuriates, in fact. How could one explain such a phenomenon? Even in a poem?

A boy leaping from his bed, entwined in a white sheet, rolling onto the floor, screaming as if the fabric were instead flames he sought to put out with his slender body.

Is this indulgence in sweetness a mark of your 20th century or is it your personal predilection, Mr. Cornell?

A little of both, I guess. Well, more of the latter, truthfully.

Cakes reign but a day, Mr. Cornell. Heed my words. But in *all* my days, I've never known anyone to refuse a Seckel pear. A ripe one too. But by the time I convince you it will be past its prime. A pity. Yes, I should have brought a Flemish Beauty instead. Or abandoned pears for apples. If only there were room to entertain inside the Blue Peninsula, we could have our fill of Seek-no-furthers: the benign equivalent of Eve's forbidden fruit, inside my private unsullied

Paradise. I do associate them with you, you know, as you have made my seeking obsolete.

A woman tending flowers from her garden: jockey club, sweet clover, day lily.

A man hurling a lovely bouquet to a startled cashier, turning what was meant to be a gracious gesture into an awkward one.

Daphne odora, lemon verbena, sunflower, star of Bethlehem.

She throws up her arms, crosses them before her face, screams. Other men race to her assistance, tackle the flower-giver.

A woman in white supine on the ground, writhing in pain, her white dress soiled with threads of red: a woman whimpering in the grass. What is it, what is it, her sister asks when she crawls home, and all she can reply is to empty a basket of daffodils, shrinking from the petals as if thorns, as if swords.

It is very strange, Mr. Cornell.

On the palms stretched out like shields, she notices each of her sister's fingers pinched as by a clothespin. Whatever could distort them so? I played scales until ravished by my piano in the woods.

My diet, I admit, causes some bemusement among my acquaintances.

I wasn't referring to that. It is your own affair, how you eat.

The 20th century, you mean, of course. It is—even to me it is strange, and I am a...temporal native. I must take refuge from it in my boxes, and I meant to give you refuge too, Miss Emily; I didn't intend for the shock of the 20th century to intrude upon your sensibility—though of course, for my own gratification, this meeting, is...something like paradise, something incredibly special, and equally mysterious.

No, Mr. Cornell, I only meant that it is strange...to be out of the house. After all these years to be in life again, and out of the house. And to speak. Already I have uttered more than in the whole of the last century. I don't know how long this voice will be with me.

I understand. I spend much time at home too, with family, do my art-work there—one of many bonds I feel with you.

You do stare so, Mr. Cornell. Do the dead look so different?

10 / 6

rectangle on the wall cast by sun somehow evocation of her presence, of her Blue Peninsula—perfect with Ravel Jeux D'eau passages on new record. good work this morning despite sluggishness after waking. bike ride afternoon? will she return? selfish to ask?

> Some things that fly there be—
> Birds—Hours—the Bumblebee—
> Of these no Elegy.

? / ? / ?

Dear friend,

   You had asked me to tell you of family, the root of which, of course, is a father and mother as husband and wife, and you, Joseph, I think, will be sympathetic to my personal interpretation: that one is married, in one sense, to moments, to melodies, to spaces of possibility, to memory, to the sound of words forming in the mouth, to the purity of a page, or, as you taught me during my sojourn in the land of Queens, to the beauty of any insignificant discarded thing.

10 / 8

up late again dwelling in conversation with Miss Emily. shape of clouds somehow appropriate for this feeling of post-intimacy. she told me, with great courage, of the period of fears and I told her of the white antelope dream so long ago at Andover and the anxiety over the study of astronomy for implications of infinity. shared many other impressions—cannot delineate in one session.

Two women huddled against one another, arms locked together, as the horse-driven sleigh glides over the hills, their crystalline laughter subsumed by the shiver of bells.

And a father's business? Obviously it is to provide for his children, and when at home to monitor their behavior—even if they would rather exhaust themselves at play, as occasionally I did, especially that one time.

A woman placing her hand over an older woman's forehead, smoothing her hair, propping the pillow upon which her head rests, then lifting her slowly, cushioning her hip, manipulating first one leg, then the other.

Brothers, we are agreed, leaven one's life with their playful humor. Where is the need for movement of limb when this agility of spirit is present? Why, for that matter, need anyone ever go out of the house?

A woman lying on the earth, under trees of chirping birds, matching every robin's trill with desperate keening.

You claim to want cake but you don't want my recipe for black cake—that I painstakingly dredged up from my memory, forgetting first the brandy, then the mace—and finally having all the ingredients in proper ratio (recalling whether more currants than raisins or raisins than currants), remembering every single one of nineteen eggs. I think you might prefer something out of that machine, something dubious and to all appearances inedible.

Insert a coin and voila! Open sesame. Imagine if the treat came shooting down like a toboggan. It's like a game, it makes me think of Coney Island, where's the harm in it, Miss E.?

A woman holding the waist of another woman, both screeching with delight as they careen down the slick hill.

And where the wholesomeness?

You are severe, Prof. Dickinson.

I am suspicious, Mr. Cornell, of magic such as this, the mechanisms of which I could not claim to understand.

Then I should be equally suspicious of your bringing me peaches from the beyond—some Eden's garden.

It was you who named and shaped the Blue Peninsula.

I shaped it of your memories. Your sentiments. And with the best of intentions. But I'd propose to you, Miss Emily, that sometimes the city's wonders are as miraculous as nature's.

I prefer the game you call "forgotten" in your studio: that dingy surface within which dovecotes reveal birds and the absences of birds. He who is gone conveys communication but leaves a hole whence he flew, and he who remains has yet to bear his missive and thus stands incomplete or unsuccessful. Why did that one make me want to cry, and still? Do you suppose those birds could send my words to Miss Barret Browning or Miss George Eliot or the Brontë sisters? Or Longfellow, Hawthorne, George Sand, or Shakespeare? Or for that matter Austin or Susie or Gilbert or Kate? And do so with dispatch?

> Some things that stay there be—
> Grief—Hills—Eternity–
> Nor this behooveth me.

? / ? / ?

Dear Joseph,

We will always correspond, for I have given you my word on it. But writing, trusted friend, to continue our dialogue, is a dangerous occupation, and letter writing, be it effervescent, is fraught with peril in its implications—as one cannot guarantee, or dictate speed of, a reply, which, until received, brands the letter incomplete, pathetic, ludicrous; whereas poems—poems one would not expect to be read by others, except, of course, those few individuals selected by the poet to receive a poem, or in the case of poems included IN a letter and written for specific occasions. It would thus seem easier, safer, to express oneself via poem, into the generous void.

10 / 11

stayed up all night rehearsing the conversation with Miss Emily. strange to think that for her, all night would not be an available unit of time, and somehow this is my doing, that for her it is always bright, always day now, and she seems content in this, but who am I to have made these choices for another person?—although I am happy that she has, in another sense, "all night" available, since during our excursion no one called her in to bed, curtailed her revels.

Just as loneliness through its regularity becomes a form of company, writing—not this sort that we do in correspondence addressed to a particular individual, but writing for oneself—writing for one's dresser drawer, you might say—precisely because it is to no one in particular, can also be a companion, a kind of appendage—something to attend to, not unlike a relative needing care, and in that sense comforting—always willing to receive one, to offer constancy, fidelity, almost like an actual place, a Blue Peninsula...

10 / 12
took the sacred Chocolate Menier wrapper and scribbled on the back of it six words: *fear, longing, loss, writing, faith, family.* how you do care for sweets! she said, turning it in her hands, and I understood this to indicate she was not willing to disclose her feelings on those precious subjects—would not acknowledge the request—not in that moment, at least.

...The same could be said of our pussy—who served often as my companion in the absence of others, who had gone out calling—purring or aloof as she'd choose, but ever available for stroking. These strokes of my pen on the page are not dissimilar in relationship; those who write should know how to recognize the purring of a page, don't you think, Joseph? The strokes could hardly be said to calm the page, but do calm the hand and mind—for we keep pets to help and please ourselves as much as to give shelter to the creatures.

Sometimes beautiful textures-—inanimate ones I mean—-can also soothe, like the lovely velvet behind that shop window, there. I should explain that I was a fabric salesman, if a reluctant one, at a company my father worked for. He designed textiles.

Your father was a man of elegance and culture, mine more a...statesman...a trustee. In any case, I was not a girl to care overly much for fabrics—preferring the raiments of the natural world or the caparisons of thought—but once I had a brown frock with matching shawl—before I wed myself to white. How long ago was that?

No mere brown wren you.

Pardon me? Mr. Cornell, if you linger before every shop window we will never get to our next destination, wherever that may be. I depend upon you to lead the way.

Oh, do forgive me, it is a habit. I only started to say, think how hard for shy folk like ourselves to peddle anything door to door, particularly art or poetry! Imagine: down the street you'd go, armed with a poem per house:
"Excuse me, I felt a funeral in my brain."
SLAM.
"How do you do? I heard a fly buzz when I died."
"Some other time, Miss."
"Good afternoon. I dreaded that first robin so."
"We dread you'll come again."
AND SLAM, SLAM, SLAM, the whole town bolted shut!

You do amuse, but disconcert me just as much with words sucked from my brain—you have so many forms of magic, Joseph. It would be very trying, I agree. At a certain point I didn't even like to answer the door of our mansion, let alone venture to the doors of others. Sometimes at night I did not care to be alone.

Vinnie, would you mind staying with me a little longer. Vinnie, are you sure the lamp is lit? It seems so dim inside. Do watch the boogers don't get in. Why not move your bed in here, dear sister—dear, kind sister?

However, Poetry, in all seriousness, is something that should only be shared selectively—very selectively. Poetry, we might say, wants to surprise someone who volunteers to be surprised. An all-out ambush makes no converts.

Miss Emily, could you trust me enough to explain...what kept you inside?

There are so many people in peculiar attire and outlandish vehicles, and all unbearably chaotic—where are you taking me? What world is this now? Oh, excuse me, it is my nerves, you must forgive the outburst.

Father, if I may interrupt a moment, are you sure the doors are locked? The windows too? I know you are busy at your study, Father; do not trouble yourself until you have finished your speech for the morrow, but before retiring, I would be greatly obliged if you would assure me....

Why *not* remain inside, when all the society I required passed through the door of my father's house—and I assure you it was highly intellectual society.

A woman laughing, hugging the waist of her partner, legs tucked up against her chest as a sled sweeps down the hill. A glancing kiss on the cheek, who knows which lips initiated—or was it the cold's kiss?—as they spill into snow as one rolling body, giddy at the bottom, giggling uncontrollably, one resting her head on the other's breast to catch her breath: "Winter is grand this year!"

I have a Bird in spring
Which for myself doth sing–

? / ? / ?
Dear Joseph,
    As to fear, suffice it to say, that which I could not yet summon the courage to say, when we were together in Queens, to you who were

both an intimate and a stranger, that all the whale oil in New England could not assuage your dear Miss Emily's fears. I required more illumination than the sun and moon in tandem to reassure me. But now you have lit the lamps for me for all eternity.

I am sufficiently at ease to offer you this frankness precisely because there are no such fears appropriate here in the Blue Peninsula—no doors, one window only, nor a conventional one, no locks, everything gives onto the sky, the heavens. There is no darkness, because the sky is confined to a square perpetually and preternaturally blue, while inside—not the blinding white of a starched sheet turned horrid beast to charge a sensitive, frightened child, but a white of powdered sugar and spirit.

10 / 13
Saturday is a mystical day. Emily appeared on a Saturday.

That night I stalked my father's house, afraid of who might enter: some booger who would more likely have regarded me the ghost!

A woman in white like a gust of wind whipping into a room filled with formally attired men and women holding dainty porcelain cups in their hands. The woman in white, despite her fleeting appearance, does not jostle the porcelain or spill the tea, seeming to evaporate as soon as she arrives. "Was that gust a ghost?" they ask the woman's father, about to make his annual speech.
"That ghost, I'm afraid, was my daughter."

? / ? / ?
Dear Joseph,

Let us always be as bold as you were on the day we met in eschewing small talk. I have thought much of family since our conversation, particularly that member named as fulcrum. It would seem axiomatic, my friend, that a father concerns himself with the wider world, and a son his immediate town, while a daughter her own back yard.

A father is one thing—a father must be about his business, to provide for his dependents, but a brother—ah, if only the passage from brother to father could be eternally suspended.

I suppose a brother with a handicap is in just such a state of suspension—he is a bonded brother, whose condition offers the beauty of never leaving, never growing apart or going away, not allowing perilous room for others to intervene. It is my private belief, Joseph, that any brother wrenched from home is neither happy nor healthy. Nor are his siblings happy. And how then can a brother leaven a family with his playful humor?

**The Past is such a curious Creature
To look her in the Face**

A brother with a handicap, I conclude, is spared the ailments that cannot help but assault him when he moves into the wider...crueler— at least more indifferent—world. How much simpler it would be to have one's limbs mimic the flower's stem—a means of attachment rather than of ambulation—just as a plant respects its roots: it would never think to journey elsewhere, unless a human hand transplanted it.

Perhaps the Lord's gift to your family, Joseph, was your brother's immobility—to spare him any such recklessness. How much simpler life becomes once one altogether abandons the notion of leaving one's house.

I know what it is like to be in a wheelchair; after I fell down the stairs toward the end of life, from top to bottom, I had to be confined to one—a humbling experience. I walked later with a cane, not gold-tipped like father's, either, not for show but function, and of course my mother was paralyzed those years, so I am not speaking through my hat.

When I fainted while baking a loaf cake, that too was strange; I did imagine I was dying. But through your genius I suspect I could have scooped the batter out, climbed in myself and made the pan my coffin! Being unacquainted with such marvels at the time, I relied upon my brother and sister to assist me in a more conventional manner.

A woman taking a paper on which she has written and folding it, inserting it in an envelope, then opening her bureau drawer and stuffing it in. But the drawer jams as she pushes it, over and over—all the other drawers of the dresser, desk, and vanity spring open like those of a cash register, releasing their contents; each time she shoves it forward another bursts open until the room is filled with papers, flying everywhere in the room, an interior Amherst blizzard.

? / ? / ?

Dear Joseph,

As to death, I have no secrets, no wisdom—nor would you ask me for such—but concerning your question of whether my poems paved the way for me, for my own dying, I can say the following: It was a terror I was primed for, if you will. Make no mistake, the act was no duplication of my conjurings on paper, but the imagination served to prepare, at least prepare the mind, for radical departure, and yet it could not, could it? Paper preparation is a flimsy one—as if having lain on one's bed could truly prepare one to lie in one's coffin!

Death was a country that I had climbed to, not toward, on a ladder of words, each word a tenuous rung—but at the topmost rung, understand, there was no true arrival; there was still up to look to, and so I did, surrounded by a vast fog. But this cloud (or shroud) did not oppress me; I was somehow not startled or disturbed to have it staring in all its immensity at my face.

But now I understand that *we* were face to face, that fog and I: having long gazed upon it, I finally recognize the mysterious face of the auctioneer of parting.

This I can describe, more easily, I think, than those fears or griefs which caught me unawares—the turning away of certain others, the changes within the household. Faith casts its beam so forcefully, univocally, on the ultimate, on life's final problem-solving, that one somehow...is equipped, whereas the smaller...merely emotional matters, quite paradoxically, might elude one, make one to feel at sea? Then compounding such confusion were the deaths of loved ones. But now, despite the inspiration for your—my—Blue Peninsula being a three-sided sea, I feel the serenity of being, rather, "at sky." As a small token of gratitude for that serenity, I will leave you with a line or two of poetry.

Estranged from Beauty–none can be
For Beauty is Infinity

And I must tell you something further, kindred spirit, brother, friend. Here in the white expanse of the Blue Peninsula, every plank in reason falls and makes no sound, and is no longer needed, as if descending into deepest softest Amherst snow.

GRID BOX

Rosmarie Waldrop

Orion, the hunter, high over my head; the Dog Star follows him through the night even though his legend is different, monstrous, two-headed. Victorian dress no safeguard against excess or waning empire. Nor can we be sure the story accurately represents the underlying power lines. A single pigeon cooing on the roof, a phallus in the void; I didn't know, she whispers, what time of day, already dark, and if my feet went to his house all by themselves.

When history is emblematic,[1] the course of ruin can be put in reverse or in the sky. A frantic innocence: a flock of doves: the virgin Pleiades. Though the abolishment of capitalism is not inevitable, fireflies next time. As if he couldn't understand, she whispers, heart in my throat, seafoam, feather on the floor, foot fetish, common-sense skin, owl or measuring eye.[2]

But the gridwork is fragile, the constellations a trick of perspective, the idea of sleep replaced by sleepiness. I prefer local intervals in ideology. And if not innocence, at least the taste of clear cold water as it comes from under the rocks. The encounter with Einstein never took place, she whispers, throat constricted, head tossed back toward the dark green feathered beauty, brought compass, sea salt, licorice, solar set, and the layered pink of the untitled palace, but forgot the question must be stated exhaustively.

This compulsion to connect the dots into story, meaning, and insomnia. The body says "I" all by itself, and history's a mishap in the statistics. Yet the obliteration of constellations by the same act that formed them is almost as radical a shock as the invention of "realism."[3] Complex, the relation between social fact and after-sex beauty, she whispers, painful secret, unusual effect, the eye in the peacock feather wet with tears, is "real"[4] a meaningful concept?

---

1. with utmost nakedness
2. partition particles
3. the dial turns, the yellow painted sun has set, a single pigeon on
     the roof
4. no known address

SONG

Robert Pinsky

Air an instrument of the tongue,
The tongue an instrument
Of the body. The body
An instrument of spirit,
The spirit a being of the air.

The bird a medium of song.
Song a microcosm, a containment
Like the fresh hotel room, ready
For each new visitor to inherit
A little world of time there.

In the Cornell box, among
Ephemera as its element,
The preserved bird—a study
In spontaneous elegy, the parrot
Art, mortal in its cornered sphere.

THE IMPETUS WAS DELIGHT
Lydia Davis

IN THE FAMILY HOME of the Baker Carpet Cleaning Company family, the box with many compartments containing the mother's heteroclite collection, waterfalls, plants, a plethora of furniture, vases, clocks, lamps, birds appearing and reappearing in motifs in the furniture and china as though alive, rapid heartbeats, Florida room, California room, Florida mug with flamingoes, the Philosophy of Fire, and the two coincided, in a moment as magical for me as, a television inset in a stone wall, a niche for a vase in a stone wall, a safe behind the back of the niche, a secret switch, a gas fireplace inset in a stone wall, objects valued for themselves, not to enhance or furnish the interior of the home but the opposite, the house extended to make room for the objects, the house too small for the objects, objects everywhere, crowded in, packed in, in a corner of an enclosed porch were many small and large china dogs, one china dog life-size next to a real dog, the real dog fat as a barrel, she has complicatedly conserved them as simply as she can, these elements of her experience, so specific, the heart of their value or the reason for their value often invisible to the general eye, the story of their finding often and readily told, explaining their value, and so long as I have these surprises, omens, five turkey vultures in a bare tree early in the morning before their first disturbance, like a doll's house furnished or overfurnished, filled or overfilled, the family home of Baker's Carpet Cleaning which has been in business 40 years, 800 lamps, vases, copper pots and pans, Teddy Roosevelt's grandfather clock, from the Psalm of David throughout, let their way be dark and slippery, they have hid for me their net in a pit, flocks of starlings passing overhead at dusk with only a *luft luft* sound of their wings, light GIANT BLUE candles, behold how good and how pleasant it is, profusion within a frame, profusion within the bounds of the house of the Baker Carpet Cleaning family, a book too within the bounds of the covers, the box of the book, the content of the book which is the fruit of concentration, condensation, of heteroclite elements, The Master Book of Candle Burning, the mother Baker's offering of a profusion of sumptuous dessert foods, cheesecake, chocolate cake, small foamy pies, chocolate candies, coming in a state of perfection magically from her kitchen, plate after plate for only a handful of guests, one family of three of large stature, one family of three of smaller stature, one old couple dressed in their Sunday best, and this is Sunday, later a pair of men, followers of the Philosophy of Fire, in the bibliography *Man and His Motives, Popular Amusements and Superstitions of the Highlanders of Scotland*, the kitchen looking out on the dining table on which sits a priceless Tiffany lamp, to the right is the copper collection hanging against the fieldstone wall, how can I burn candles, neologists and others who should be in a position to know, it is in the mother's house that you will see all these wonderful things, things that the mother recognized as wonderful, worth so many thousands or hundreds of dollars, of $$$, at first appearing to be plain, low-priced items, of magnificent value now recognized, out of the crowds and hosts of low-priced items at a flea market or a yard sale, a low-value vase, a low-value lamp, an ebony carving, the grandfather clock of Teddy Roosevelt, which is the star attraction, in Scotland to ward off witches, among the Parisees by a newborn baby, fire temples on a hilltop and the faithful worshiped in the open air and licked up the water that was in the trench, many people keep a vigil light burning constantly in their homes, all things were made by Him and without Him was not anything made that was made, Sunday is yellow, Monday white, Tuesday red, Wednesday purple, Thursday blue, Friday green, Saturday black, In the Shadow of the Bush, she rakes out the fire and drenches it with water, she then cuts off her hair, a crossed condition, Weed of Misfortune Brand Candle, Confusion Brand Oil, White Power Brand Candle, Domination Brand Oil, they are as stubble before the wind and as chaff that the storm carrieth away, sputtering candle a prediction of misfortune, the energy and intensity of these Bakers, mother and son, their glistening eyes, their enthusiasm leading and serving heteroclite handfuls of guests walking with respect from room to room, slow, gingerly, their eyes stopped at each packed cabinet, a clock-lined, clock-topped chest, an inlaid chest, a room full of ebony, the father before his death was the builder, the father built walls of stone, made a fountain to run down the wall of the old living room, the first living room, then the mother wanted a larger fountain, and the father built another living room onto the back, right around the backyard barbecue fireplace, turning that into a hearth, and built a larger fountain now surrounded by a host and crowd of illuminated plants beyond an ebony wild pig, an ebony boar discovered at a flea market when the mother spied the one tusk sticking out from under a truck, the boar was offered for $50, worth so many hundreds of $$$ now, if two leaves of Basil are placed upon a candle and burn away quietly the marriage will be happy, manufacturers of automobiles, cosmetics, dresses, etc. use colors which please and soothe, this *leaning toward* a color, Astral Colors, these would be your PRIMARY CANDLES, available in authentic Astral Colors, an exaggeration of any house for ordinary living though they do live here, or just the mother lives here, so many seats, so many cupboards, more than one living room, so many cups, dishes, pictures, sofas, chairs, tables, splayed legs, drawers, leaves, knobs, aprons, whatnots, dropleaves, crosspieces, pins, butt hinges, clocks, cockleshells, cabriole legs, acanthus leaves, palmettes, splats, volutes, arm stumps, S-scrolls, vases, plants, crystal, stone walls, carpets, so much glass, profusion, proliferation, around every corner more profusion, their eyes stopped, their eyes resting here, there, high, low, Gold (Yellow) the Color of Attraction, Magnetic Hypnotic, Captivating, Drawing, Fascinating, Persuasive, Charming, Alluring, Cheerfulness, applications for Fire Worship based upon research by no less an authority than W.S. Blackman, in this era of modern homes it is not practical to utilize open altar fires, to Learn the Truth, to Relieve Pressure by an Enemy, some time ago I heard of the account of a young woman who felt pangs of Fear, she had so many doubts about her ability to keep a job, to keep her husband's love, she felt that she was being harassed by unseen, hidden forces, out of his holy hill, Selah, the lifter up of my head, thou has smitten all my enemies upon the cheekbone, thou hast broken the teeth of the ungodly, ninety percent have amatory diffi-culties, try this, a small supply of Frankincense and Myrrh, one can-dle of each color should be lighted each morning before going to look for a job, the law of Moses permitted altars of either clay and earth or of stone, ALWAYS USE VEGETABLE OIL CANDLES, the first man is of the earth earthy, as is the earthy, such are they also that are earthy, as we know, there is but one true Altar, and that is our HEART, his hands full of sweet incense beaten small, and bring it within the vail, the mercy seat that is upon the testimony, set aside a place in the home that is quiet, attic, basement, playroom, bedroom, spare room, a beau-tiful altar of which you can be proud, many people believe that all that is necessary is to procure a candle of the right color and light it and then every dream and wish will come true, it is not as easy as all that, FIERY WALL of PROTECTION brand OIL, DOVE'S BLOOD brand OIL, BIBLE brand OIL, COMPELLING brand OIL, INFLAMMATORY CON-FUSION brand OIL, dressed with UNCROSSING brand OIL, 30 min-utes each evening before retiring, the use of SYMBOL candles is strictly an American custom prevalent in certain of our Southern States but now also found in Detroit, Philadelphia, St. Louis, and many cities and towns between, molded in the shape of an animal, such as a cat or lion, in order to understand the symbolism involved it is necessary to go to the Dark Continent, strange and weird rites of African Medicine Men, the accomplishments of these individuals, the story of the brutal Congo trader, the native workmen, unable to endure it longer, sent one of their number, the idol in question was still on the dresser but THE HEAD HAD BEEN SNAPPED OFF!, the mother saw the value of them within their form apparently of low value, bergere, cabriolet, recamier, canapé, settee, club chair, chesterfield, the mother went with a girlfriend to the field of stones to find the right stones and bring them home, they made many trips at dawn, the father built, the mother and father went to the old buildings in the city as they were being torn down and went inside to buy pieces of the old buildings, an ironwork partition, a neutral tone the color of pale coffee is said to be the most desirable, CONFUSION brand OIL, each day a chapter of the Song of Solomon will be read with all candles burning, although war is perhaps the most ungodlike expression of the human race and is in itself an irreligious activity, during Time of War, in short, he is King to his Queen in the Kingdom of his Home, but when a man is called to war there is a definite letdown, those remaining behind turn their faces heavenward seeking Calmness and Dynamic Power, those who follow the Philosophy of Fire have delved deep into historical archives, half-forgotten practices of the Ancient Zoroastrians, though a nominally peaceful people, did have their wars, he would guide his spirit to Paradise where it would forever be engaged in the conflict with evil and the ultimate victory of Ahura-Mazda, in the center is placed a GIANT EVERLASTING TYPE CANDLE, an even larger candle is available that weighs 13 pounds and burns for TWO YEARS, CON-QUERING GLORY brand OIL, the following verses are read either by the soldier or by someone whom he designates, fight against them that fight against me, let their way be dark and slippery, they have hid for me their net in a pit which without cause they have digged, neither let them wink with the eye that hate me without cause, against them that are quiet in the land, the precious ointment upon the head that ran down upon the beard, that went down to the skirts of his garments, for about 500 days (or nearly 1 year), some tantalizing vision of some happier hunting ground, the novitiate will at first stumble upon many obstacles unless he or she first acquaints himself with certain fundamentals of the Art, the Rituals can be a delightful occasion or a confused muddle, a hopeless waste of time, the guests that are invited are customers of the Carpet Cleaning Company, who have had their carpets cleaned by them, they come into the house shyly, it is especially beautiful at Christmastime, because of all the Christmas decorations and the special arrangements of the mother, who has fashioned little snowy scenes involving miniature fir trees and figures skating in circles on glass lakes, penguins or little men and women, who do not stop going round and round while the guests walk through and stop to sit and talk and eat cake, or sit at the bar and eat chips and nuts and drink an alcoholic drink, the guests are dressed nicely, it is Sunday, the house is a single-storied ranch house among other ranch houses on small plots on a street called Pine Street, immediately inside the front door is Teddy Roosevelt's grandfather clock and following it the ebony room, ebony table, ebony cabinets, little sculptures of ebony, value is high in $$$ but those $$$ are for reasons of historical interest and fine workmanship, no deviation was permitted, it is now realized that they must be modified and adapted to meet the needs of individuals living in a fast-moving world, the Zoroastrians could not go out to a corner store, available from reliable Supply Houses, SPARK of SUSPICION brand Candle (Brown), RADIANT HEALTH (Red), WEALTHY WAY (Green), GLOW of ATTRACTION (Gold or Yellow), BENEFICIAL DREAM (Lavender), SATAN-BE-GONE (Orchid), LADY LUCK (Gold), WEED of MISFORTUNE (Black), when you order from your dealer always give your date of birth and let him select your Astral Candle for you, with such branded candles you just cannot go wrong, of the HAND FIXED type, many people start each *new* ritual for each *new* purpose with an entirely *new set* of candles and this truly is the most logical procedure to follow for it insures an altar of outstanding beauty and dignity, if a Blue used candle that had been dressed with a particular oil were reused later for another purpose *the symbolism would*

be lost because of the improper dressing, purchase one of the Basic
Candle Burning kits, the guests do not know one another, they are
introduced and sometimes talk to one another, but are not expected
to talk and are free to stand and eat a piece of cake off a plate or to
keep wandering, a billiard table around in back of the stone hearth, a
secretary desk, an escritoire, an ebony serving man, an ebony black
serving man, meridienne, banquette, pouf, ottoman, ear, stile, cross
rail, stretcher, cross stretcher, crinoline stretcher, cornice, top rail, dia-
mond point, hanging stile, bracket base, frieze, frame stile, the value
is in their being what they are, not in their meanings, door panel, peg,
chiffonier, column, bobeche, globe, tureen, every cause has its effect,
the blackness of night offsets the light of day, certain cults of mad
adventurers who attempted to rule the people, these religious racket-
eers, the infamous Black Mass, degraded nature and base hideous-
ness, for example, muddy brown-green, greenish yellow, purple red,
very dark brown, midnight blue, black, etc., all such Magic is based on
the Law of Sympathy, ran a needle through his head, or where the
heart would be located in reality, wax from a deserted bee's comb, if a
hunter drives a nail into the footprint of an animal, a dirt highway
winding twelve miles, when his feet were wrapped in his coat he was
WALKING ON HIS OWN PROPERTY, Darkest Africa, missing things of
a most personal nature, Dame Fortune seemed to frown upon his
every activity, a rival had taken the things, robes worn by ancient
priests, etc., in this position was placed a clipped piece of sock, glove,
shirt, hair, toothbrush bristles, evil influence dominates the scene,
Master of his own Destiny, said to give off depressing vibrations,
BRING CONFUSION OR TO EXERT PRESSURE ON ONE'S ENEMIES,
Midnight Blue Inflammatory Confusion brand Candles, move candles
closer to the center each day, WHEN TWO ARE IN LOVE WITH THE
SAME PERSON AND THE STUDENT WISHES TO ELIMINATE THE
RIVAL, Glow of Attraction brand Candle, when two people are after
the same job, Green Crown of Success brand Candle dressed with
Crown of Success brand Oil instead of the Glow of Attraction brand
Candle, to be read: the 93rd Psalm, platter, rim bowl, creamer,

ramekin, pepperpot, saltcellar, gravy boat, pitcher, jug, blade, bolster, ferrule, point, slot, prong, root, your author has dug deeply, everything new in it is old and everything old in it is new (animal fat excepted), a folly like Hearst Castle, like the Winchester House, this can be a highly subjective (personal) business & yet a means of attempting expression of communication, water running down the wall, a couch formed of concrete, these seven fundamental rules are simple and easy to follow, the more progressive individual may create his own particular symbolism, early and late the appreciation of the acquirer was the desired reward, each guest was given a pretty-colored gift bag upon departing, containing a white unglazed ceramic Cupid for an adult, a bright chrome car for a child, from the yard to the porch to the kitchen, said Joseph, don't think we're working on my work, fixing lunch, raking, banking, running to town, Bohack's, after a while they took their lunch and tea breaks together, they enjoy a wide sale among reliable Supply Houses, so noble a custom, TO SETTLE A DISTURBED CONDITION IN THE HOME, Peaceful Home brand, and he shall be like a tree planted by the rivers of water, first o'week coming upon an abandoned house with no KEEP OUT signs, it is on a main artery but protected by a hedge, unlike the side (open) approach, a smashed-up commonplace affair but an intriguing challenge, not one of the older places, TO OBTAIN MONEY, mine own familiar friend which did eat of my bread hath lifted up his heel against me, TO WIN THE LOVE OF MAN OR WOMAN, in position X may be placed a photo of the loved one if one is available, a mixture of Frankincense and Myrrh may be burned, TO CONQUER FEAR, Crucible of Courage brand Candle, Psalm 31 in its entirety, be thou my strong rock, for an house of defense to save me, pull me out of the net that they have laid, thou hast considered my trouble, thou hast set my feet in a large room, I was a reproach, I am forgotten as a dead man out of mind, thou shalt keep them secretly in a pavilion, and the proud doer, sit with Joseph in the back yard, many times he would eat a meal consisting entirely of desserts, I know these things, but it is not necessary to know them to enjoy the postcard, Rockefeller Center, Christian Science, TO

CHANGE ONE'S LUCK, Astral Candle of person who is object of wrath, Spark of Suspicion candle dressed with DOMINATION brand OIL, ORCHID Candle or Satan-be-Gone candle dressed with UNCROSSING brand OIL, Conquering Glory candles, collecting loved or desired things and putting them together in some kind of order within a frame, or excess, or jumble, lumber room, disregard position A as this applies to Exercise 17 only, each evening for 15 days or until satisfied, time and again, beehive forests and thimble gardens, as skillful as he was, the recipients, he did not share the accepted conception of the limitations of time, the past for him was not something that continually receded, it was as available as the present, home poor heart, marvelous and ordinary, available in 14 colors, note the two-color effect and speckles, available in authentic colors, TO HEAL AN UNHAPPY MARRIAGE, Astral Candle of husband dressed, Astral Candle of wife dressed, Fire of Love candle, should be moved two inches daily in direction of arrows, the Song of Solomon, TO OVER-COME A BAD HABIT, to symbolize the bad habit undressed, for he shall pluck my feet out of the net, what she thinks is valuable, what may be valuable and what may be worthless, cheap, ugly, or valuable, worth a great deal, beautiful, or valuable only to her and her family because they are her creation, the skaters on the pond made out of a mirror, skating over a magnet and a motor, or what is valuable to more than one, to many, to the world, two inches daily in direction of arrows, repeat until satisfied, TO STOP SLANDER, Candle of Petitioner, before retiring until satisfied, FIERY WALL of Protection, Mandrake root in a saucer or incense burner, thou shalt break them with a rod of iron, thou shalt dash them in pieces like a potter's vessel, if the Success deals with MONEY use GREEN Candle or WEALTHY WAY, FORTUNATE DREAMS—Lavender or Beneficial Dream, in his yard bunny statues wandered, organic matter moved itself along but he tended to the decay of organic matter, pound cake was brought to harden in the sun, pears became softer and softer and more liquid by the day, it does not pay, it was not intended to pay, its air, full of music, is a fog that turns from brown to yellow, from yellow to white, sunrise and sunset, his hours, compounded of foreign woods, the impetus was delight, gifts without the recipient's knowing their origins, Red Candles or Radiant Health dressed with Crucible of Courage Oil, TO LEARN THE TRUTH, TO BRING CONFUSION TO ANOTHER WHO IS THOUGHT TO HAVE CAUSED UNFAVORABLE VIBRATIONS, let them be turned backward, let them be turned back for a reward of their shame that say, Aha, aha, TO BREAK UP A LOVE AFFAIR, and he heard me out of his holy hill, BLACK Crucifix Candles dressed with XX Double Cross brand Oil, Red Candle UNDRESSED to symbolize sterility or barrenness, DO NOT move candle 4, thou hast broken the teeth of the ungodly, TO SOOTHE AND QUIET THE NERVES, Astral Candle of person in nervous condition, the enemies of the Lord shall be as the fat of lambs, they shall consume, into smoke shall they consume away, the Psalm should be read slowly and with careful attention and should be accompanied by a state of calm meditation, the steps of a good man are ordered by the Lord, and he delighteth in his way

POEM IN WHICH A BIRD
DOES SOME OF THE TALKING
John Yau

Why wasn't I invited to grip the balustrade?
Am I not made to strut across the scene?

Hasn't the sunset already entered the library?
And hasn't it closed the door to anyone

who was anxious to file me away?
White, oblong, upright—though not a book,

the thick-sided box is both a prison
and an immense stage,

which allows your fans to adore you
as you make your grand entrance,

then pirouette, like a clock in a wet railway station.
I am a humble example of something—

I'm not sure what—
the next civilization no longer appreciates.

Next door, a silent movie, its hypnotic subtitles
serenading the startled brow of the story's heroine,

Paved Honey, best known for her
inventive outbursts of wickedness.

Why doesn't the audience see the ropes
hoisting me to my rightful place in the sky?

We were unable to leave town
before it was overrun

by a tumultuous outpouring
of brightly costumed insects,

some of which we barely manage to name.
Carnivorous birds remain our only consolation.

We keep them beside us, in hotel rooms.
Believe me when I say I wanted to write sooner,

but nothing eventful has transpired
since I sent the last postcard to show

you a photograph of The Bridge of Slobs
before it finally collapsed

beneath the crowds dancing on its neck.
If there is a small pleasure

to be found in any of this,
I have nearly an eternity to find it.

IF THE AGING MAGICIAN SHOULD BEGIN TO BELIEVE

Jonathan Safran Foer

If the aging magician should admire the ribs of his hungry gondolier, it's only because they look like wands. His breath had steamed the front window of a curiosities boutique once: suspended in a refrigeration unit was a wand, into whose length was carved: *Congealed Blood of Baudelaire's Swan*. In the back of a rare bookshop, he once found a threadbare quarto—the pages dissolved in his hands like cotton candy in the mouth—that told of a wand in Greenland, assembled from the vertebrae of a virgin princess who died of anxiety in a high tower, still clutching the white hanky to her flutterless heart. A friend of his—no, not a friend, exactly, but a man with whom he drank milk during a break between symposiums at the *Magic in the Age of Efficiency* conference—said he had a wand so heavy it could never be lifted, and one so light it refused gravity's lingerie. But he'd never seen or heard of a rib wand. And certainly not Venetian.

You do not eat much? he observes in his pidgin Italian.

I do not believe in food, his hungry gondolier replies, propelling the thin boat on.

No?

The gondolier sends his gaze over the horizon.

Well, I believe in food, the aging magician jokes, clapping his hands, *and I'm going to eat your city into the ground! Pizza! Pizza! Pizza! Every meal and then some. I deserve it. Do you have any idea how old I am?*

If like a mime in love at dusk the aging magician should feel a profound urgency,

it is his need to reconcile himself with his life before he forgets all of his most convincing tricks, it is the emergency of his Parkinsonian hands and the black hat's stubborn false backing, it is the anxiety of fakery: He wonders if he has lived, perhaps, a very normal life, or worse, a bad life, or, worse, has not lived at all, but performed a long series of tricks. What, after all, is the sum of sixty-five hundred invisible birds?

It is essential, now, to remember why he did the things he did in life, what goals he gave himself. He needs—*needs*—to remember where it was, sixty years ago, that he wanted to be in sixty years. Without remembering, he can't know if he is there.

Did I want to be famous? Did I want to have many lovers? Or one great love affair—the love story of the century? Did I want to be popular? Did I want to be mean, sometimes? Funny?

Because I am not famous and have had neither many lovers nor the love story of the century—unless the century was such that its love story could be an unfulfilled one. I was never particularly popular. I was rarely mean and rarely funny. If this is what I intended, then my life has been all that I wanted it to be.

The aging magician would examine his hands
while the mother tried to pull the children loose from the jungle gym.

This was his ritual before every show, and it may have harkened back—or so he occasionally thought—to the womb, when he encountered his hands for the first time.

No conspicuous smudges or scrapes. No filth lining the fingernails. No rings. His veins had risen to the surface of his skin, and nothing could check the stubborn shake of his left hand: the involuntary gesture summoning that final muse of illusion. (It's said, in professional magic circles, that all *real* magicians are left-handed. How it pained the aging magician, then, when his tremors forced him to learn to handle the wand with his right hand, to pull the blue parakeet from the thimble with his right hand, to palm the cork balls with his right and unnatural hand.)

He would file his nails to the quick, as he did before every performance, pull the crown from his watch (freezing time for the duration of his show, which would be, now, no duration at all), brush the few remaining strands of white hair over his head, fumble with the cinch of his tea-stained cummerbund, lick moisture across his parchment lips (emptying his mouth of moisture, which required, in turn, a withdrawal of moisture from the lips), and attach his glasses to his face with a tan rubber band around the back, insuring that they would never fall off in the middle of a trick.

You are an artist,
he would tell himself. *You perform magic for children for their amusement. You have succeeded when the illusion is carried out flawlessly and the wonder sustained. This makes children amused; it makes them believe in things that don't exist and are better than those things that do. This is what you are paid to do, and this is your calling.* He would check each of his tricks twice, as was his ritual, to make sure that nothing misbehaved when called upon to amuse and transcend. (Amusement, for the aging magician, *was* transcendence. Not cheap and kitschy games, not giving *scissors* a hard *c*, as other, so-called, magicians did, but *real* amusement: the urgent need to know how something is done, but not wanting to know. *Transcendence*, the aging

magician thought, while trying, with no success, to tie his bow tie, *is the sum of two contradictory urges—needing and not wanting. It is a sadness we can live with.*)

The ball in the ball in the ball was ready. The hanky's secret pocket was still there, as was the black hat's stubborn false backing. He made the coloring book go blank and then, with a different riff of his thumb, fill with colors. Yes. It still works.

He always half-expected to find that the tricks themselves had vanished, leaving only an ordinary ball, an ordinary hanky, an ordinary black hat, a colorless coloring book: that the magic would one day undo itself as its final trick, leaving only *things.*

Your city is beautiful, but

don't you think it might be a little less stinky without all the water? Which is another joke, of course—another lost in translation. *The older I get,* the aging magician thinks, *the less I am understood. The movement toward death is one toward complete misunderstanding.* He cannot help but imagine it as a chart:

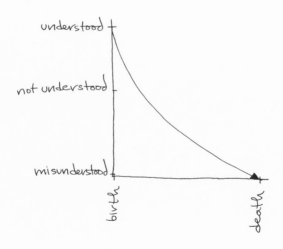

But maybe, he thinks, it's the other way around. Maybe I have been getting better at expressing myself. Maybe my new silences are more accurate than my old words, and when my eyes close for the last time— the open-ended silence—I will be understood completely. He sees it:

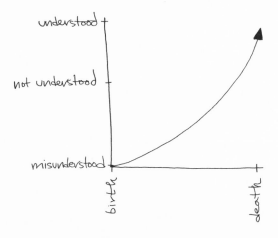

Or perhaps I have never been understood at all, not a single word or gesture, except, that is, for the moments of love:

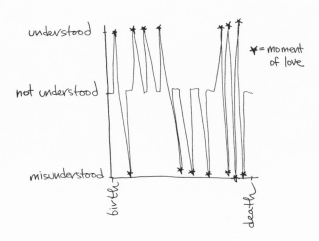

He starts to repeat himself, fearing that the gondolier didn't hear him: *Your city is beautiful, but—*

I do not believe in beautiful things, the gondolier says, lifting his long, skinny arms above him, letting the breeze blow across his chest like a sculptor's gaze. *Only in beauty.*

The aging magician kneads his left hand with his right one. *What a strange thing you just said! And what faith! I admire you greatly, gondolier, for your strangeness and faith. You do believe in admiration, don't you?*

But he doesn't answer. He shows no indication of having understood, or even heard, a word that the aging magician has said. He gives the magician no reason to take his own existence for granted, or the existence of the gondola, cutting the green-brown water, or that of the water, holding the city in its net, or of the city, holding the water in its net. *What if,* the aging magician wonders. *What if the world, which we cannot help but think of as being an intricate order of nets—the cloud is held in the atmosphere's net, the rain in the cloud's net, the hydrogen and oxygen molecules in the net of water's compound, the fallen rain in the sidewalk's net, the sidewalk in the net of the earth's crust, the earth's crust in the net of the planet, the planet in the net of the solar system, and so on—is not that way at all? What if the fallen rain holds the sidewalk, and the planet the solar system? What if when I pick up a baby, take it to my chest and cradle its head under my palm, it is the baby holding me? Or worse—it is unthinkable!—what if there are no nets at all, and I am not holding the baby, and the baby is not holding me?*

Upon searching the pockets and false linings of his jacket, the aging magician finds a rip, whose purpose he searches his brain for, until he realizes that it is only a rip,
like the small and hopefully unnoticeable one behind the knee of his tuxedo pants, and the one out of which his big toe sticks. It's true: his magic garments are falling apart. But there is nothing to be done. He

can't afford new ones, or to have these fixed, and his shaky hands would be worthless with a needle and thread even if he knew how to sew. There is another rip just below his right elbow. He fingers a rip where his right shoulder meets his collar. A rip—he will soon be all pockets and no pants—at his left shin. A rip, it's impossible to ignore, across his sleeve. To conceal some bunch of crushed-velvet roses? No. He had fallen in front of his building after a show and had had to tip the doorman his night's earnings to be picked up silently: the feeble are not allowed in his building, and the aging magician doesn't want to go to a home for the feeble, even if that is what he needs.

He looks into the eyes of the elderly on the street, on the bus and in cafes, and wonders if they are performing the same trick. He looks at those in middle age, between parenthood and grandparenthood, already gray but not yet stooped, and wonders if they, too, are magicians. And what about the young? Those still in the first half of life? Are they like him? Are they older and sadder and weaker than they appear? He sees a beautiful young girl get off the subway and follows her through the city. Is she happy? Is she healthy? And children and babies? He hopes that they are only what they are. *Yes*, he thinks, I *want people to be what they are, and all other things to be what they are not.*

I don't believe in magic, but I do believe in you,
a young birthday girl told him after one of his last shows.

Thank you, Princess, he said, taking her fingers between his hands. *What a lovely thing you just said!*

Your tricks were all really bad. I saw the thin string between your hand and the cork ball. She giggled. *I also saw that your hat had a thingy in the back, because when you weren't looking, one of my friends took it and showed us. That's where the bird went.*

Oh, the aging magician said, removing his top hand from the little girl's, still holding it beneath. But his *Oh* was accompanied by a wooden blue parakeet that flew to the Princess's ear, pinched her lobe in its beak, licked it, and whispered, *I was trying for so much more.*

And the square marbles? he asked.

My father has that trick. But this *My father has that trick* was accompanied by a wooden blue parakeet that flew to the aging magician. It nestled its head deep in his ear, as if trying to push its way inside of him: *I love you more than anything in the world, even my father.*

I'm so sorry, the aging magician said. *I've ruined your party.*

No, she urged, blowing wisps of brown hair from in front of her eyes. *It was funny. I loved it, and so did all of my friends. That's what I came to tell you. No one really believes in magic, anyway.*

And that's why I never had children,

the aging magician once told his doorman, whom he sometimes referred to as his assistant: *because I never had a wife.* The doorman listens to the aging magician; he humors him—partly out of sympathy, knowing he is the only one the aging magician has to talk to, and partly for the secret tips—but he doesn't care. The aging magician is a sweet old man, he thinks. He thinks: It must be very hard.

Maybe that's why I became an artist of magic in the first place: to be around children. I came close to marrying a woman once. We were very young then. Younger than you. We followed her father's map to a winding creek on the far end of their property. I brushed my teeth three times that morning, and asked her to wear that blue dress I liked so much, which she did, but without shoes. And even without shoes, she looked fully done up. That's the kind of girl she was. We made it there as the stars were beginning to come out of the trees. I got down on one knee—I can't even get to my knee anymore!—and said, "You know that I love you, but what you might not know is that I've always loved you, even before we met. The love between us was contained entirely within me, and always will be if you say that you don't love me. I will be like a man in an airport, carrying the luggage of a lover he can't find."

He lost himself in thought.

Let me give you a piece of free advice, he said to the doorman:

Make for yourself a world you can believe in.

It sounds simple, I know. But it's not. Listen, there are a million worlds you could make for yourself. Everyone you know has a completely different one—the woman in 5G, that cab driver over there, you. Sure, there are overlaps, but only in the details. Some people make their worlds around what they think reality is like. They convince themselves that they had nothing to do with their worlds' creations or continuations. Some make their worlds without knowing it. Their universes are just sesame seeds and three-day weekends and dial tones and skinned knees and physics and driftwood and emerald earrings and books dropped in bathtubs and holes in guitars and plastic and empathy and hardwood and heavy water and high black stockings and the history of the Vikings and brass and obsolescence and burnt hair and collapsed soufflés and the impossibility of not falling in love in an art museum with the person standing next to you looking at the same painting and all the other things that just happen and are. But you want to make for yourself a world that is deliberately and meticulously personalized. A theater for your life, if I could put it like that. Don't live an accident. Don't call a knife a knife. Live a life that has never been lived before, in which everything you experience is yours and only yours. Make accidents on purpose. Call a knife a name by which only you will recognize it. Now I'm not a very smart man, but I'm not a dumb one, either. So listen: If you can manage what I've told you, as I was never able to, you will give your life meaning.

If the gondola's rigid seat—the armchair lacquered in coffin-black and dully black- upholstered—is the softest, most luxurious, most relaxing seat imaginable,

it is because the aging magician cannot remember a rest so peaceful. *You have a most lovely gondola,* he turns to tell the gondolier, but his words come out as nonsense—or not nonsense, exactly, but song. Musical notes. The hungry gondolier remains silent, pushing on. The black water parts like thighs in anticipation of the gondola's prow. It whispers to the aging magician: *Shhhhhh. Shhhhhh.* He leans forward, lies on his side, curls up his feet, puts his ear against the gondola's floor. *Shhhhh. Shhhhh.* It's like listening to a soon-to-be-mother's belly, he thinks. *Shhhhh. Shhhhh.* Serene and peaceful. Safe. He will not get hurt now.

I'm sorry, the aging magician sings, ear to the gondola's floor, *but where are we?*

Who paid the aging magician towards the end: nobody.
So he did parties for underprivileged children. It was the only way he could remain with the service that hired him out and the only way he could continue to practice his art. His powers of illusion had declined—he could remember only the two simplest of his card tricks, and was entirely unable to make things reappear after having them vanish. At best, he was a second-rate magician. Obvious. Sentimental. Hands too unsteady for any sleight. It was worse than embarrassing.

The children had to finish many of his tricks, when he forgot the ending, or his hands wouldn't cooperate. *Ta-da!* a young girl would say, pulling the blue parakeet (*his* blue parakeet) from the thimble as he seated himself behind his cabinet of enchantment. And when he didn't have the strength to pull the mile of rainbow ribbon from his mouth, a young boy came to his aid.

His shows became more like magic clinics than performances—*This is how it works; This is how it works*—and after each he would weep (always disappearing behind his enchanted cabinet so that the children wouldn't see him), for he knew that

If a magician gives away all of his secrets,
he is no longer a real magician.

The new parties took the aging magician to poor neighborhoods, where for birthdays parents would draw lipstick circles around their eyes and call themselves clowns.

We're so glad to have you, they would tell him as he unpacked. *It's truly generous.*

The shows were much shorter (as the aging magician had fewer tricks at his disposal), and the illusions less impressive, but to his surprise the wonder multiplied: both the children's and his. For the children, the excitement lay in not knowing how, or even if, the trick would be completed. *Can he do it? Is it possible?* For the aging magician, tricks became what he always wanted them to be for his children: objects of enchantment. After vanishing a rabbit and forgetting how to make it reappear, he would look at his hands, he would search them for gadgets and wonder, *How did you do that?* And when the parakeet flew the thimble, leaving only a single blue feather on the ground as proof that it had once existed, the aging magician asked, *How? How? How? Tricks, all of them. I know. I performed them. But what were the tricks? And how can I know that I will be able to repeat them?*

The aging magician wonders: *Is the universe a pocket, or a rip?*

It is late already, and he knows he should go home before he catches a cold. But the sky holds his gaze; the stars do. He thinks thoughts that are so complex they suggest simplicity, so simple they demand complexity: *I am looking at stars that might or might not be there.* Because: *It takes time for light to travel.* And: *Everyone looks at the same stars.* But: *Everyone looks at them through different eyes.* I wonder: *Are the stars held in our eyes, or the other way around? Could the eyes of the living form a net, in which everything that exists is held?* Which would mean, therefore, that: *Everything that is not looked at is not held in the net, and so does not exist.* He sees it:

Or: *Perhaps the universe is the net, and human eyes are like marbles in a mesh bag. Those eyes not in the universe's net belong to those never to be born.*

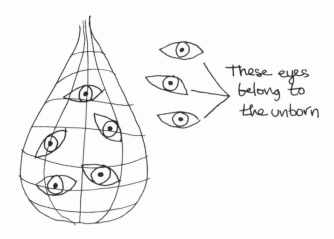

    Is the universe a pocket, or a rip? Is the blackness a secret lining? A false backing?

    He feels a shiver dance up his back and can hear a voice telling him it's time to go home.

Hey, the boy says,
stopping the magician in an alleyway between Chinese restaurants.

He grabs the aging magician's skinny forearm, which is so skinny that the boy can feel his fingers through it, as if he were squeezing air. *Give me your money.*

I don't have any, the aging magician says.

I don't believe you.

But look, he says, showing the boy his wallet (out of which falls a blue feather), *nothing.*

The boy leads the aging magician behind a dumpster and makes him undress, one piece at a time. He searches each of the magic garments. *Tell me where it is,* he says.

I don't have any.

You're hiding it. I know you old people.

The magician takes off his black jacket (with the half-pulled-out stitches of an illegible name across the lapel), and his ruffled blue shirt with blue ruffles. There is only enough change for the bus. At the boy's command, he takes off his ripped black slacks, revealing bony legs spotted with brown blotches.

Come on, old man, the boy says, *give me your money.*

I told you, I don't have any. I—

Suddenly, the aging magician is aware of the boy's tremendous youth and beauty. Long arms and fingers. Full lips. Moist. Those eyelashes, the aging magician imagines, could hold thimbles of water. His skin is perfectly smooth and taut. Everything the color of health. No, not health, exactly, but portraiture. Wasn't there a famous painting of this boy in one of the far rooms of the museum? His left arm poised like a serving platter, his head tilted to one side, everything soaked in blue, wasn't that the one? What did the plaque beneath it say? *Portrait of a Petty Thief as a Young Man*? No. *Beautiful Boy Bathed in Blue?* Notice those irises, so delicate, so wet and feminine. Those teeth, so precisely crooked, stained by a master. If he isn't a painting in the museum, then he must be, himself, a museum— exhibiting his life's work in his leather gallery, the curator of his own portable retrospective.

The aging magician is overcome—*I want to be like that*—and for the first time he feels that his fear of death is far more refined, more convincing and familiar, than his love of being.

Come on, the boy says, pounding his foot against the pavement, *please, just give it to me. Why are you doing this? Just give it to me.*

You are so beautiful, the aging magician wants to tell him. *Do you have any idea how young and beautiful you are? No, you can't, of course. One is only able to see the things that one doesn't have, that one is not.*

The boy searches the magic garments again, while the aging magician stands nearly naked in the cold, goose bumps coming forth from his arms like signs of the zodiac. It takes the boy several minutes to look through all of the secret pockets. He pulls out two clay pipes that the magician hasn't been able to find, and thirteen silk handkerchiefs, and four hundred yards of multicolored cellophane ribbon, and eighteen thousand invisible birds, whose existence no one would have any reason to believe, or, for that matter, doubt. He even turns a cork ball into a soap bubble, without knowing how. *Amazing*, the aging magician says, his ribs supporting his chest like tent poles, like wands. And the boy, unable to subdue his boyishness, says, *Tell me how! Tell me!*

If the aging magician should begin to feel like the king's food tester, it's because he senses that everyone is looking at him out of the corners of their eyes, waiting for him to die. *Now? Now?* He walks to the supermarket for his pumpkin seeds and pineapple soda, and everyone, he's sure, is stealing glances to see if he's still alive. *Now? Now?* On the way to the zoo, where he watches children watch the animals watch the children watch the animals, the gaze bouncing back and forth forever—one of the saddest, most uncrossable distances. (He wishes they could talk to each other!) As he waits so patiently outside the theater for a glimpse of his favorite coryphée, who never comes. In the Automat, eating pastries heavier than the sum of their ingredients.

Even the doorman, he thinks, has been looking at him funny. They all want to know if he is still alive.

While the aging magician has never believed in God, and isn't about to now, he knows that God is the king for whom he must die: that his death will preserve some greater life. The poison, this time, is grief, and God has sent him to eat its tasty morsels before they reach the dark and starry platter. Or maybe what he fears is just the opposite: that nobody is looking; that his death, like his life, is without purpose; that there is neither greater good nor evil—only people living and dying because their bodies function and then do not; that the universe is a rip.

If aging magician should begin to wander bad neighborhoods like dime and junk stores,
it's because he is looking for the boy who robbed him of nothing. He wants to find and protect him, hold him in time.

Beautiful, he whispers, wandering back alleyways with his shaking hands in his bottomless pockets. *Where are you?* He asks the man with the cloudy eye at the gas station. He asks the double-dutchers and brown-bag alcoholics. He asks the young girl who sits always on the same stoop, whose lollipop never dwindles.

Do you know of a boy around here? He is about this tall, and has very long arms and fingers. His eyelashes are also very long. He is a thief. But not a petty one. A real thief.

No, they tell him every time. *Never seen anyone like that.*

But you must. (He doesn't believe them.)

No, mister, every time. *I don't know who you're talking about.*

He takes his hanky—his functional hanky—from his pocket, and draws on it. *His arms are like this,* he says.

And his eyelashes are like this. When you approach him, you think you're walking through a haze, but it's his eyelashes.

Never, they say.

He goes, whispering.

If the aging magician should forget where it is he's going,
he tells his hungry gondolier: *You lead the way.*

Where was it that I meant to be? How did I get to this particular city? Why am I here? I remember telling you about my vacation, but I don't remember ever deciding to take one, or packing any bags—no, I never packed a single bag—or boarding a plane, or saying good-bye to my true love (whom, after all these years, I have still yet to find), or any of the children for whom I have turned all of those marbles into blue parakeets and then made those parakeets vanish like the memories of dreams.

Why didn't I notice the speed with which we have glided through this city? Would it have made the trip impossible? Why is it most impossible to notice the things that you will most regret not having noticed? Is that what noticing is? Is that what regret is?

I feel so heavy: like the moment before sleep, when all of the world is possibility and the only thing I want is rest. I remember as a child needing to fall asleep and not wanting to fall asleep. When I battled against sleep, whom was I battling?

Where are all of the people? I want to be with people and I am alone. Where are the opera houses and fish stands? Whores and glass blowers, eunuchs, moon-scrapers, tutus and heavy pastries? Where are the marble miles, the grime-stuffed flutes, the swans in the mire?

O, it's true, my hungry gondolier, isn't it? Those aren't white sequins in the tooth fairy's tiara.

It's true: Only the blind can have sex without pain.

It's true: We're not blowing kisses to the minaret's barred window; we're going to burn down the palace.

It's true: Adults cry less than children, and have more need to cry.

It's true: When you care about me, you care about you caring about me. And when I care about you, I care about me caring about you.

It's true: There's gold at the end of the rainbow. That's all there is!

It's true: I can no longer distinguish my pockets from my rips, my tricks from being tricked.

It's true: I have been to this place before.

You propel us on, and without turning to face you I say: *I don't trust you.*

You have understood me, because from over my shoulder I hear: *It doesn't matter.*

If the aging magician felt, for a long moment, more alive than undead,
it was only because he saw the boy again, drinking a black cherry soda in front of the dime store, painting the straw blood-red with his breath. The aging magician followed him when he began to walk, vowing not to lose him this time, not to take him for granted.

He followed the beautiful young boy through a maze of side alleyways, past the fried coconut stands, over the crumbling bridge under which cardboard houses leaned and fell, around the decaying monuments and dry fountains, along the bank of the filthy river, which stank like dying animals. He kept a distance, not having the courage to make himself known, to say, *You, most young and beautiful boy, do you remember me? Tell me that you do, even if it's a lie. It's a lie I'm now ready to believe. Let me know that I made some impression on you, that I changed your life in some small way, as you have mine. Touch me, lie to me. We could remind each other of who we are not.*

The boy kept walking. Faster now. The aging magician was sure he was walking faster than the boy, but the distance between them never shortened. Their strides seemed perfectly timed, no matter how the magician pushed himself, so that the boy was never within, nor out of, his reach. *Beautiful, beautiful, beautiful,* he whispered, and began to run, but they remained evenly spaced, as if the boy were pulling the magician by a string, or the magician were pushing the boy with a pole. *But I am no threat to you. You could level me with one hand. I have no weapons. I don't want to hurt you, or scare you. Please. I just want to look at you. Please. See me in you. See you in me. Help.*

If the aging magician's hands should begin to shake more vigorously now, summoning the illusion of life and reality of death, trying to encourage his own belief in himself,
then he is dying.

I don't want to die,
you say, but the hungry gondolier pushes on, propelling the boat faster through the narrow channel.

I'm so afraid of dying.

Nothing can make up for a life without belief, says a voice from the back of your head. The gondolier?

But I don't believe there are things to believe in. Everything is some sort of trick.

Of course.

Then what could I have ever believed? you plead, anxiously fingering your ribs.

That's not my business, he says.

Help me. I'm afraid. Once you die you are dead forever.

This is true, he says.

I don't want to be dead forever.

Because you haven't had time to do what you wanted to do with your time?

Yes, you say. *I need more time.*

You know that I love you, but what you might not know
is that I've always loved you, even before we met. The love between us was contained entirely within me, and always will be if you say that you don't love me. I will be like a man in an airport, carrying the luggage of a lover he can't find.

Who are you?

What do you mean, Who am I?

I'm sorry, but I think you've got me confused with someone else.

Don't you recognize me?

Are you OK?

Why are you doing this?

Doing what?

Recognize me!

I don't know you.

I love you, and you love me.

No. I'm sorry.

Recognize me!

If the aging magician should know that he is about to die—he was always about to die; we are all, always, about to die!—
he will surround himself with children: the rambunctious five-year-old who ate so much frosting while helping his mother bake his birthday cake that he vomited blue on one of the aging magician's birds; the sweet baby sister of a birthday girl, with wet eyes and thin hair; the eight-year-old girl, who did or didn't exist, who kissed him on the cheek after his show and said, *I don't believe in magic, but I do believe in you;* the son of the famous playwright, in his thick black frames and braces; that girl he fell in love with, who came upon him weeping after a show and offered a thimble of coconut sherbet, saying, *Maybe you'll*

feel a little better if you made this disappear; the babies, the toddlers, the five-, six- and seven-year-olds; the children too old to have a magician at a birthday party, and too old to have a birthday party, and too young not to believe in magic, and too young not to have a birthday party; the children he didn't father, the children he wasn't, the infinity of possible lives that slipped through the mesh of the universe's net. They will come to his side as he dies on that hard hospital bed— hundreds of children, like birds to bread, thousands of them, ready to take him to the slit in the sky, hundreds of thousands of them.

AMERICAN ASSEMBLAGIST, collage- and toy-maker, film pastiche artist, correspondent, and connoisseur of trinkets Joseph Cornell was born on Christmas Eve, 1903, in South Nyack, New York. The blissful childhood that would become the inspiration for much of his recollecting and work ended when his father died of leukemia in 1917, leaving the family with tremendous financial burdens as well as the task of caring for Cornell's younger brother, Robert, who suffered from cerebral palsy. Thanks to his mother's insistence on education and belief in the arts, and to her numerous part-time jobs, Cornell was able to attend Phillips Academy in Andover from 1917 to 1919, where he studied, with no particular success, sciences and Romance languages.

Between 1921 and 1931, Cornell hawked fabric samples in Manhattan's manufacturing district. It was during this period that he had his first contacts with the New York art world, attending ballet and opera performances, frequenting gallery exhibitions, and avidly reading literature, poetry, and art history. This was also when he began rummaging through dime stores and rare book and junk shops. He amassed a prodigious archive of objects and images that would later become the source material for his boxes and collages. Perhaps in the spirit of this exploration and transformation, Cornell converted to Christian Science.

Through a fortuitous meeting in 1931, Cornell became acquainted with gallery owner Julian Levy, and within a year several of his two-dimensional collages appeared in an exhibition of Surrealist art at the Julian Levy Gallery. Over the next several years, Cornell experiment-ed with, refined, and perfected his medium of box construction, first using boxes that he found or bought, and later making his own. He did all of his work in the basement of the house he shared with his mother and Robert on Utopia Parkway, in Flushing, Queens. As his reputation spread, his boxes began to appear in galleries all over New York. At the same time, he wrote and created several films. He also became a kind of reclusive vertex of the art world, hosting Marcel Duchamp, Max Ernst, Matta, and several other important Surrealist and non-Surrealist painters, writers, poets, and—his favorite—ballet dancers.

In the late 1930's, inspired by the bird cages hanging in the win-dow display of a local pet store, Cornell began his aviary series, one he would work on until his death. The boxes, which at first featured only parakeets (cutouts from natural history books and children's shooting gallery sets, mounted on conforming pieces of jigsawed wood), would soon include owls, cockatoos, canaries, and finally, about a decade later, an absent bird: an empty perch in a barren cage. Cornell's birds were often world travelers who pasted collage remnants of their exploits on the walls of their cages: hotel paraphernalia, foreign news-paper clippings, European advertisements, theater and dance pro-grams. They were alter-egos of Cornell himself, who, because of his need to care for Robert and help support the family, didn't venture outside of the New York City area after his Andover years. The birds left traces; Cornell gathered traces together.

Cornell continued making and exhibiting his poetic theaters, concentrating on such themes as ballet, astrology, mathematics, soap bubbles, Medici prince and princesses, hotels, and children. Even though he eventually achieved international acclaim, the inability of art critics to group him with any of the prevailing movements that developed in the art world during the period of his long career— Surrealism, Abstract Expressionism, Pop Art, Minimalism—made his place in the canon precarious and unique. (Compared to an artist like Warhol, Cornell acquired relatively little fame, and a tremendously adamant following.)

His brother Robert died in 1965. His mother the following year. While his work output then declined, he hired assistants to help scavenge for and construct his boxes, and he still corresponded with a large number of people—including his deceased brother and mother, for whom he would continue to buy gifts. Cornell's final musem show was, at his request, given for children. His boxes were displayed at an appropriately low eye-level, and chocolate cake and cherry soda were served in place of canapés and champagne. He died in his home, December 20, 1972, of heart failure.

DIANE ACKERMAN is the author of seventeen works of nonfiction and poetry, including, most recently, *Deep Play* (prose) and *I Praise My Destroyer* (poetry). In honor of her work as a naturalist, she has the rare distinction of having a molecule named after her (dianeackerone).

>-+→-o-←+-<

MARTINE BELLEN is the author of *Places People Dare Not Enter*, *Tales of Murasaki and Other Poems*, which won the National Poetry Series, 1997, and *The Vulnerability of Order*.

>-+→-o-←+-<

JOHN BURGHARDT is a poet and short-story writer. He teaches high school English and lives in Bethesda, Maryland.

The winner of the Rome Prize in Literature, MARY CAPONEGRO is the author of *Tales from the Next Village*, *The Star Café*, *Five Doubts*, and the forthcoming *The Complexities of Intimacy*. She teaches in the MFA program at Syracuse University.

ROBERT COOVER is the author, most recently, of *Ghost Town*, *John's Wife*, and *Briar Rose*. He teaches electronic and experimental fiction writing at Brown University.

LYDIA DAVIS's books are *Break it Down*, *The End of the Story* and *Almost no Memory*. She is currently working on a new translation of Prousts's *Swann's Way*.

SIRI HUSTVEDT is a poet, fiction writer, and essayist. Her books include *Reading to You*, *The Blindfold*, *The Enchantment of Lily Dahl*, and *Yonder*.

Poet, art critic, and MacArthur Fellow ANN LAUTERBACH is the author of numerous books, including *On a Stair*, *Before Recollection*, *And for Example*, and *Clamor*. She teaches in the MFA program at Bard College.

BARRY LOPEZ is the American Book Award–winning author of *Arctic Dreams*. Among his many other books of fiction and essays are *About This Life* and *Light Action in the Caribbean*.

<hr/>

RICK MOODY is the author of the novels *The Ice Storm* and *Purple America* and a collection of stories, *Demonology*, among other books.

<hr/>

BRADFORD MORROW received an Academy Award in Literature from the American Academy of Arts and Letters in 1998. Author of the novels *Come Sunday, The Almanac Branch, Trinity Fields, Giovanni's Gift*, and the forthcoming *Nambé Crossing*, he is the founding editor of *Conjunctions*. He teaches at Bard College.

<hr/>

HOWARD NORMAN is the author of the short-story collection *Kiss at the Hotel Joseph Conrad* and the novels *The Northern Lights, The Bird Artist*, and, most recently, *The Museum Guard*. He lives with his family in Vermont and Washington, D.C.

<hr/>

JOYCE CAROL OATES is the author of a number of works of fiction, poetry, and criticism, including, most recently, *Blonde*. She has been the recipient of the National Book Award and the PEN / Malamud

Award for Excellence in Short Fiction, and is Professor of Humanities at Princeton University.

><+>+O+<+><

DALE PECK lives and works in New York. He is the author of *Martin and John*, *The Law of Enclosures*, and *Now It's Time To Say Goodbye*.

><+>+O+<+><

ROBERT PINSKY, United States Poet Laureate 1997-2000, is the author of six books of poetry, most recently *Jersey Rain*, five books of criticism, and numerous translations. He teaches in the graduate writing program at Boston University and is the poetry editor of *Slate* magazine.

><+>+O+<+><

ERIK ANDERSON REECE is the author of *My Muse Was Supposed to Meet Me Here* (poems) and *A Balance of Quinces: The Paintings and Drawings of Guy Davenport* (criticism). He lives in Lexington, Kentucky.

><+>+O+<+><

JOANNA SCOTT is the author of five novels, including *Make Believe*, *Arrogance*, and *The Manikin*, and a collection of short fiction, *Various Antidotes*.

ROSMARIE WALDROP is a poet, translator, and novelist, whose most recent books include *Reluctant Gravities* and *Split Infinites*.

PAUL WEST is the author of twenty novels, most recently *OK*, about Doc Holliday, and *The Dry Danube: A Hitler Forgery*. The government of France recently made him a Chevalier of the Order of Arts and Letters.

DIANE WILLIAMS's most recent book of fiction is *Excitability: Selected Stories*. She is the founder and editor of the new literary annual *NOON*.

JOHN YAU is a poet, fiction writer and critic. He also writes extensively on contemporary art. His works include *My Symptoms*, *Edificio Sayonara*, and *Hawaiian Cowboys*.

Joseph Cornell

HABITAT GROUP FOR A SHOOTING GALLERY

1943

15.5 x 11.125 x 4.25 in.

wood, paper, glass

Photograph by Michael Tropea, Chicago

No reproduction without express permission

Purchased with funds from the Coffin Fine Arts Trust;

Nathan Emory Coffin Collection of the Des Moines Art Center, 1975.27

Joseph Cornell

UNTITLED (DETAIL)

c. 1950's

18 x 12.25 x 4.75 in.

box construction

Photograph by Bill Jacobson, courtesy of PaceWildenstein

Private collection

Joseph Cornell

UNTITLED {PAUL AND VIRGINIA}

c. 1946-1948

12.5 x 9.9375 x 4.375 in.

mixed media box construction

Collection of Robert Lehrman, Washington, D.C.

A Convergence of Birds

Original Fiction and Poetry Inspired by the Work of Joseph Cornell

Design and typesetting: Anne Galperin
Production Manager: Craig Willis

Composed in New Caledonia {Adobe Systems}, with display lines in
ENGRAVERS ROMAN {Bitstream} and ENGRAVERS {Monotype}.
New Caledonia is a contemporary typeface based on the typeface
Caledonia, which was designed in the late 1930s by the esteemed
American graphic designer William Addison Dwiggins. Engravers is
a traditional typeface most often seen contributing its dignified style to
paper currency.

Printed in Hong Kong

Manufactured through Asia Pacific Offset

This book is printed on acid-free paper.
Text pages: 118 gsm U.S. Woodfree
Tip-on illustrations: 128 gsm Japanese gloss.

Tip-on Regal Printing

Bound by Regal Printing

ISBN 1-891024-22-1
Edition of 5000 trade copies

ISBN 1-891024-30-2
Edition of 350 signed by the authors

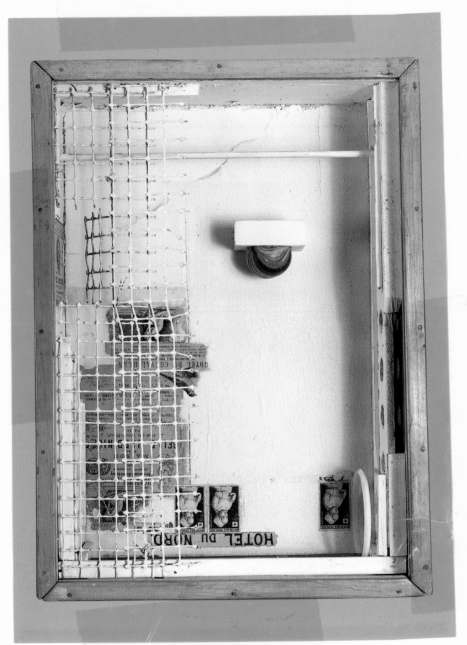

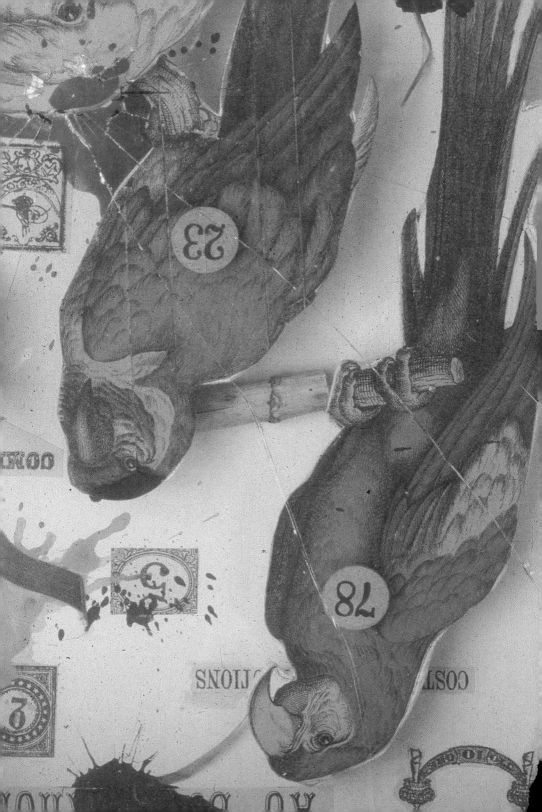